Magnificat

B53 053 101 X

D1375100

Marilyn Edwards

with illustrations by France Bauduin

Catnip

To Mary, our mother, with love

CATNIP BOOKS
Published by Catnip Publishing Ltd
Quality Court
off Chancery Lane
London WC2A 1HR

First published 2013
1 3 5 7 9 10 8 6 4 2

Text © 2013 Marilyn Edwards
Illustrations © 2013 France Bauduin

The moral rights of the author and illustrator have been asserted
All rights reserved. No part of this publication may be reproduced,
stored in a retrieval system, or transmitted in any form or by any means
electronic, mechanical, photocopying, recording or otherwise, without
prior permission of the copyright owner

A CIP catalogue record for this book is available from the British Library

ISBN 978-1-84647-147-6
Printed and bound by CPI Group (UK) Ltd, Croydon, CR0 4YY

www.catnippublishing.co.uk

PART I

PART II

PART III

ROTHERHAM LIBRARY SERVICE	
B53053101	
Bertrams	24/05/2013
JF	£6.99
MAL	

PART I

1

THE TOWN

The little cat picked her feet up high as she stepped gingerly through the snow. As she licked the last trace of gravy from her whiskers, she flicked her magnificent tail back and forth across her back. Cat was unaware of the story that the tipped-over dustbin lying behind her seemed to tell and as she sauntered close to a line of parked cars, the memory of the snatched feast she had just eaten made her huff out a sigh of contentment.

'Oi – you!' A man's voice boomed across the street. 'Yes – YOU! I'm talking to you, you little toe-rag! What d'you think you're doing?' And with that the man started to run straight at her. 'You filthy little scavenger, you're no better than a rat.'

The cat stood still, frozen in fear, her happiness gone. What would this aggressive monster do once he reached her? And why was he shouting? She cowered down, put her ears back and spat at him to show him how fierce she was. It didn't work. As he lunged out to grab her she gave a drawn-out hiss of fear, and, snakelike, she slunk down low, crawling under the car parked next to her. From there she crept along to the next car and then the next. Cat felt safe close to the warm metal hulk. She liked cars. Ones that weren't moving at least. The ones that raced past on the road definitely didn't make her feel safe. She could see the man's feet two cars away. He had stopped walking. One boot was tapping up and down impatiently and her keen hearing picked up the sound of his fingers drumming on the roof of the car.

The little cat edged backwards until she reached the last car in the row. It was, she decided, not at all a good place to be. This one was really horrible. It was hot and cold all at the same time. It had been driven recently and the pipes were hissing hotly causing great dollops of slushy ice to plop down on her back. As she sat there cars whooshed past noisily on the road, large and fast and very close to her head. The little cat wasn't used to the hustle and bustle of traffic. It felt dangerous – and the air around her was filled with the bad smell that came from cars making her feel slightly sick. As she continued to hide, she licked her nose nervously.

Her mind returned again to the remains of the burger that she had found lying by the side of the bin, half hidden in the snow. She had been hungry and her recent diet of spiders had not been very satisfying. Finding that burger had not only filled her stomach but left her feeling more able to cope with anything life now had to offer. Whatever animal had knocked over the bin hadn't been at all thorough at rootling through its contents. But it hadn't been she who had knocked it over and spilled its contents, she was far too slight for that. Not that she could explain this to the shouty man, who seemed to think she was the one who had done it. Or perhaps he always shouted at cats whenever he got the chance? Better check where he was.

Cat roused herself to peer anew under the line of parked cars. The boots were no longer visible. She crawled out from under the car and scented the air. The man had gone. She opened her jaws wide and yawned in relief, leaving the ghost of her breath hanging in the air above her head. She stood up and had a long stretch. A sudden flurry of snow borne on the cold November wind stung her eyes and made her shiver as it found a patch of wet fur on her back. She sidled into a sheltered doorway and sat down to give herself a quick lick.

Snow was a new experience for her as she was only half-grown and this was her first winter. Earlier this morning, when Cat first stepped out into it, she had caught her breath in fear. It was shockingly cold and wet, and since its silent fall the scents that she relied on to tell her everything she needed to know about where she was and how secure she was were deadened by this strange covering. She felt unsure of where it was safe to go. She had been walking around in it all morning and the pads of her feet were starting to sting and now, licking herself clean, she could taste the bitter salt mixed up with the sand and grit that lay all around the town on roads and pavements alike.

Having satisfied herself that all trace of salt had, for the moment, been licked away, her good spirits returned to her.

She stood up, quivered her great tail high in the air, scented the wind, and started to trot briskly through the little town to see what delights might lie in store. Her progress was repeatedly interrupted. She kept picking up smells that told her how recently this dog or that cat had passed by and it all took time to absorb. Twice she had to make a quick dive into a doorway as the rumble and sound of the traffic simply became too much, rattling past her head so fast. This was the first time in all her life that she had been in a town and, when she wasn't busy jumping out of her skin from fright, its bustle and odour intrigued her. The thunderous main street, where all the traffic gave off such smells and vibrations, frightened her, but as she turned into the quieter back streets, whose narrow cobbled ways seemed somehow safer, the little cat felt a rising sense of excitement at the prospect of a new adventure.

At the only home she had ever known, where she had lived since kittenhood, there had been one main road with intermittent traffic, but nothing she had ever seen had prepared her for this astonishing townie racket with all these cars and buildings and people. At home there had been quiet fields teeming with small furry creatures just waiting to be caught and – once in a while – a friendly neighbourhood cat would come and pass the time of day full of benign curiosity.

Her thoughts of home were interrupted by the sight of a door opening a few yards ahead of her. A long slim hand came down and placed a bowl of cat food on the pavement, almost in front of her nose. The door clicked shut. The little cat was astonished. Could this food be for her? She stopped and licked her nose nervously, then, slowly, she stepped forward and smelled it. She started to eat, quicker and quicker until . . . she felt a presence and turned, swallowing quickly. There, a short distance away, was a large female tortoiseshell cat, whose tail was thrashing the ground with a force that spelled nothing but trouble. As the little cat stared, the bigger cat edged towards her sideways, one foot crossing menacingly over the other, while a low growl rumbled from deep inside her.

The smaller cat instinctively flattened herself and collapsed on her side submissively, but too late. The tortie towered over her, tail whipping from side to side, ears back, hissing, before she shot out her front paw, claws fully extended, slashing the younger cat's face, catching her ear and the skin near her eye. Blood ran freely from the wounds and the younger cat shook her head violently to try to throw off the sting. She rolled over to get out of the way and mewled a long '*mnnnnnnn*' in a plea for mercy. As she struggled to her feet, the little cat knocked the bowl over and what little food was left dissolved darkly into the slushy snow. Cat kept her head down and avoided eye contact with her opponent, instinctively knowing that to appear meek would be the only way to avoid further injury.

The older cat instantly recognised that she held the position of strength and drew back. As the tension died down, the door of the house opened and a tall woman bent over to peer at the upturned bowl. She saw the young blood-streaked cat cowering in fear, but the resident tortie had disappeared. The woman stamped her foot crossly making the intruder cower more, and started to shout.

'No, no, no, no, no. That food wasn't meant for you. It's not yours. Go away, go on, scram!' And she picked up a big broom and started to waggle the bristles right in the little cat's face. Cat backed away in alarm and, turning with her tail arched in a loop between her legs, she galloped off down the cobbled street and round the corner as fast as she could run.

Once round the corner Cat settled down for a thorough groom. Having spent long moments repeatedly licking the side of her left paw until it was quite wet, she gently used her whole front leg again and again, lick, wipe, lick, wipe to sponge away the blood from her torn eye. Having done that to her satisfaction she then gave the same treatment to her ripped ear. As she cleaned the wounds it hurt a little and she purred to herself for comfort as she groomed and slowly she became calm. Satisfied her wounds were clean and the bleeding was no more, Cat rose, ready for action, and started to walk.

The network of cobbled streets finally led her into the Main Square – an area without cars. As she looked around she saw that there were benches around the edge and a small clock tower in the middle. Cat found herself drawn to some steps near a drinking fountain and trough. There she sat down to watch, partly concealed by a large bin. People came and went. Some of them sat on the seats and threw bread for the birds. Cat watched the people, but she felt strangely withdrawn from them and being semi-concealed they took no notice of her.

People here seemed to be quite different from the folk she'd met at home; they were cross and shouted a great deal and waved brooms at her for no reason. Even other cats were altogether less friendly. Cat sat quietly with her thick tail wrapped neatly across her feet. The only outward sign of her concentration was the very tip of that tail, which twitched with an apparent life of its own as her attention shifted from the people, to following every jump and flutter of the birds as they jostled for food. She licked her nose with controlled excitement. The birds interested her mightily. Later, after the people had moved away, she wandered across and chewed up a small piece of the bread that the birds had missed. It wasn't very satisfying and the taste was dull. Odd that they liked it so much. Some primal instinct told Cat that birds would taste a lot better than the stuff they ate.

As night fell she returned to the empty garage where she had spent the night before – her first night in the town – and settled down to sleep. Her mind was jumbled with the many images and smells and sounds of all that had happened this day. As she curled up in the old armchair with the stuffing bulging out, her thoughts drifted back to how she came to be here.

Cat had arrived in this town in a most uncomfortable manner and completely by accident. It had never been her intention to leave home. Her downfall had been her passion for cars and vans. From the time she had first started going outside she adored to climb into cars, or indeed any vehicle. She liked the smell of them and the warmth and shelter they provided when you got inside them. And that was how she had ended up here. A van had been parked outside her house, with its rear doors invitingly wide open. In the blink of an eye she had leaped up into it and found a large round bucket with a cosy rope curled up in the bottom. After snuggling inside, she was sound asleep when she heard the doors bang shut. As the engine started up she miaowed out as loudly as she could manage, but she couldn't get through the wire grill that separated the back of the van from the front, where the driver was. She had been trapped in the back for an age, during which she was rattled around and jerked from side to side. Sometimes the van stopped and she kept hoping the rear doors would be opened, but they remained firmly shut.

At long last the van came to a halt and everything went quiet. After a bit of a wait, the driver came to the back and opened the doors and the little cat, giving one long drawn out '*mneowwww*' of relief, sprang out into what had become the dark, cold world of a winter evening far from home. She heard the man yell after her, but she'd had her fill of that van and shot down a side alley. Cat scrambled under a gate and, after checking the driver was no longer in pursuit, she had found this old, damp, smelly garage.

And here she was for the second night running. The garage doors were locked shut, but there was a crack at the bottom of the ill-fitting door and it was through this that she had come and gone. She had made her bed in an old armchair with a strange-smelling squishy sort of cushion that had half its insides spilling out. She had kneaded it fiercely over and over again until she'd made a hollow that was the right shape for her body.

On her first night, while she had slept totally exhausted, undisturbed by anything, great flakes of snow had fluttered down silently all the night long and by the morning everything outside in the Town she had yet to discover was covered in a thick white blanket making it more mysterious still.

Now, as she curled in a tight ball for warmth, she thought longingly of the home she had left by no will of her own. It

14

had been warmer by far and a lot more comfortable than this garage and the people had been gentle and kind, giving her regular meals. Cat sighed and turned again to try to get more comfortable. Slowly sleep enveloped her, but as she slept, she mewled out, repeatedly, in distress. She was never to remember what it was that was so upsetting her, but if anyone had peered through the grimy windows they would have seen her feet twitching and her whiskers moving frantically.

2

THE DOG

Ben's young face was tense with anxiety and his forehead was etched with deep worry lines as he slammed out of his house. The cold air hit the boy with force, making him gasp. He hesitated and, turning, he opened the door again, remembering the coat on the back of his chair. Immediately he thought better of it and banged the door shut even harder this second time. With his back to the house he balled his right fist violently into the palm of his left hand, moaning loudly in frustration. Ben felt so angry he wanted to cry – not that he would give in like that. But it simply wasn't fair, it really *wasn't*.

Ben started to walk, kicking an already-battered cola can further along the gutter. The wind made him shiver violently and his nose started to run. He wiped it with the back of his sleeve. Without his coat, gloves and scarf the cold was going to win. All too clearly he could imagine his mother taunting him with, 'And whose fault is that?' He screwed up his eyes, then opened them again quickly and shook his head to reject her imagined chiding.

What Ben needed was to talk to someone. Someone who would understand. Someone like Josh. By now, on autopilot, he had started to cut through the alleyways of the housing estate. But as he got closer to Josh's place he started to think . . . What would he say to Josh? And how would his friend react? Thinking about it made his head throb. But it was impossible not to – think about it, that is. It just kept churning away inside his brain. Ben walked faster. He wanted to get away from all that shouting. Away from home. Away from everything.

It had all started because he'd made the mistake of asking Mum if there was the slightest chance that he might be given a dog of his own for Christmas. He knew it was only the end of November, but you had to start working on these things early. You'd think he'd asked for a herd of elephants, white ones, with diamond-studded toes, the way she went on. She made it seem like it was the most unreasonable and selfish thing anyone in the world had ever asked for, instead of a perfectly normal request. Josh – after all – had a dog. All his friends had dogs, well most of them did and if they didn't they had other things, like guinea pigs – or really cool things, like snakes.

It was after the mail arrived that things went belly up – and then some. It had been *awful*! He shuddered at the memory and took a quick breath to calm himself. Ben had still been trying to list the reasons why a dog for Christmas was a good idea as his mother opened the post. She had been looking at something when suddenly she stopped and just kept saying the same thing, over and over again. 'What on earth is this? What IS this?' Then she was waving some sort of statement under his nose and shouting at him – really screaming – the same questions over and over again. Not that she gave him a chance to read it. All Ben knew was that he was being grilled Big Time about her credit card.

He'd panicked. His mouth went dry and his brain blanked. She kept waving the sheets of paper under his nose and pointing at one line asking for an explanation but not waiting for one. Then, suddenly, she went quiet and slumped down over the table like all the stuffing had fallen out of her and she sobbed – deep, racking sobs.

The crying was worse than the shouting. And then there had been her voice. It went all low and angry in a way Ben had never heard before.

'You wait. I'm telling your Dad about this. I mean it, Ben. This time you've really gone too far. It's too much. I can't cope.' Her voice caught and she started a long coughing fit. Ben's dad lived miles away, over the hills in Yorkshire, and neither of them had anything much to do with him. He couldn't imagine what Dad would say or do, but the fact she was going to tell him was definitely not good news.

And that wasn't the end of it.

'By rights, I should call the police. You're nothing but a hooligan.' That awful low voice again. 'No, worse! You're a rotten, grubby thief!'

Ben had caught his breath in a shocked hiccup that sounded

a bit like 'What?' He couldn't believe what she was saying, but he didn't know how to defend himself. No words came to him. His mother paused for a long time looking down, then she raised her eyes and stared straight into Ben's. Tears were flowing down her face but she remained silent. Ben blinked as he felt his own eyes stinging. He chewed the inside of his lip. It wasn't like that, what he had done – was it? It wasn't *that* bad. It couldn't be. She'd got it all wrong. She must have, but even as he thought about it now, Ben couldn't make sense of any of it. Not even the angry little knot of guilt he could feel forming in his stomach.

As Ben rang the bell at Josh's house he heard Clueless, their yellow labrador, barking a warning – or possibly a welcome, it was hard to tell the difference with Clueless. There was an enormous hubbub the other side of the door. Ben hugged himself as he heard barks, claws scratching on lino, skidding sounds and shouts as Clueless did his famous skateboarding trick on the rug towards the front door, anxious as always to be the first one there. Sure enough, there was a loud thump as dog and rug hit the door together. Ben heard Mrs. White's voice announcing she'd told him that's *exactly* what would happen and the door was opened with a flourish and Josh's mother stood there, pink-cheeked and laughing.

She had her finger hooked through the dog's collar, but on recognising Ben she let him go free. Clueless sprang up at the boy in front of him and washed him from top to toe with a long wet tongue smelling of hot dog-breath. Ben laughed in spite of himself and, wiping his face dry, he crouched down to put his arms round the dog's neck. He turned his face towards Josh's mother, mouthing the question '*Josh?*' as Clueless continued to whine and slobber over him excitedly.

'Ben – hello! And the answer to your question is: where else but on his computer upstairs.' Josh's mother grinned and stood back to let Ben pass her. 'I honestly don't know what you lads find to do on those computers all the time, it's not as if you're doing anything useful like the household shop or something!' Ben winced at the mere mention of online shopping and thumped upstairs. He pushed open Josh's bedroom door and flopped on to the bed, followed by Clueless who, panting amiably from the effort of being a dog, jumped up and sprawled out next to him.

'Hey, Ben! Just hang on a sec can you?' Josh threw over his shoulder, eyes fixed on his game. But Ben couldn't hang on and started gabbling about how Third World War had broken out in his house. Josh paused his game and turned to watch his friend, listening, gripped, as Ben got to his mother's accusation about the credit card. By now Ben was petting Clueless for his own comfort, rather than the dog's.

'What made her think it was you who spent the money?' This innocent enough question from Josh prompted Ben to twist the dog's ear, making Clueless whimper in protest. Ben felt strangely unhappy about telling Josh all this, although he wasn't sure why, since Josh already knew most of it.

'Apparently on her bank statement it actually gave the name of the website, which was a bit of a giveaway. But, Josh,' Ben paused, ' . . . well, the thing is, when I was doing it, it was so difficult. I had to try three times before I could make it work, and when it did work I couldn't face doing it again, so

20

I took a full year's subscription in one go.' Ben's voice went a bit quiet so he was nearly whispering. 'And it came to sixty-nine ninety-nine.'

Josh whistled. 'That's a lot! No wonder she noticed!'

'When you're online doing that stuff, it's so easy once they accept the card. You just click, click, click and everything works.' Ben grinned mischievously, but Josh just nodded.

'It was weeks ago that you joined, wasn't it? You seemed to have had that cyberdog of yours for ages,' Josh said. 'What was the name of the website?'

'Oh, it was called *my imaginary pet dot com*,' Ben replied. He stood up and stretched, yawning lengthily. 'It seems to have taken forever to show in her statement.'

His grin faded and his brows furrowed together. He turned away so Josh couldn't see his face.

'But, Josh, I haven't told you what she's done. It's hideous. I can't bear it.' Josh leaned forward to try to see Ben's expression. Ben moved across to the dog again, keeping his head low. 'She's banned me from the internet. Completely. For ever!' Ben buried his head in the dog's neck. He wanted to cry, but of course he couldn't. In a muffled voice he said, 'As I was leaving the house she shouted out that she was changing the password and when I get home I won't know how to get in any more until she tells me I'm allowed to use it again.' Ben knew it wouldn't be for a long while.

'What you going to do about homework?'

'Dunno. I suppose she'll have to explain to school. I can't bear it. Then everyone'll know.'

Josh said, 'Hey that's rough, that's really rough. But I'm sure the ban won't really be for ever!' Ben nodded, but it wasn't the schoolwork that was on his mind. He looked across at his friend with a tragic expression on his face. He could feel the wretched tears pricking his eyes again and, turning away, he blinked hard and swallowed repeatedly until he was sure they had gone.

At that moment Chloe, Josh's twin, came into the room telling Josh that their Mum needed them. As brother and sister ran downstairs Ben turned back to Clueless and hugged him until the dog groaned. Ben adored this dog, but privately thought that the name Clueless was a bit unfair, although everyone in Josh's house thought it was really funny since he really was – Clueless, that is. So when Ben finally got himself a virtual pet on the website he had been tempted to call it Clueless before he realised how wrong it was.

He wanted his newly acquired 'pet' to be with him always, to go with him everywhere. To never leave his side. So the name was obvious: Shadow. Ben desperately wanted to explain to Josh why not having Shadow any more really was the end of the world, but he didn't know how to start. Ben felt he actually lived through Shadow. When he was on the website he felt free – he and his dog could roam wherever they wanted. When he so much as thought about Shadow he felt connected in some way. He could imagine the presence of Shadow in the room, almost. But it wasn't the same without knowing that he was there, inside the computer, waiting for him.

He'd known that asking his mum for a real dog for Christmas was always going to be a really long shot. His mum did cleaning jobs, but he knew there wasn't much money and dogs needed a load of upkeep – feeding, vet bills – as well as lots of looking after. But with one blow, because of that stupid credit card, it looked like he was now going to be without both a real and an imaginary dog. It just wasn't fair. However, Ben consoled himself, at least Shadow would still be waiting for him when his internet ban was over.

Ben heard Josh walk back into the room and he decided to try to make his friend understand.

'The thing about Shadow is that he never says I'm wrong, or complains about things or nags me or anything . . .' Ben's voice faltered and ground to a halt. As he looked up he discovered that not only was Josh in the room but so was Chloe – with a big grin on her face.

'Wow, whoever you're talking about sounds too good to be true!' Chloe said.

'Well he's not!' Ben retorted hotly and Josh threw a pillow at Chloe, pulling a face at his twin to shut her up. But Chloe's interruption made Ben retreat further into himself. Out of nowhere Ben could hear an irritating voice in his head chanting *blood is thicker than water*. With Chloe around, did Josh really care whether Ben was there, or what problems he had?

His thoughts were interrupted as he heard Chloe reminding Josh that their mum had asked if Ben wanted to stay for tea and, if so, they needed to have it now, because she, Chloe, had to go down to the church. With that she left the room and thundered down the stairs. Josh looked across at Ben questioningly as he started towards the door in his sister's wake.

Ben suddenly felt he couldn't face everyone over a happy family meal, so he mumbled vague thanks and explained he really needed to get home. Much was on his mind and, increasingly, on his conscience and he knew he had to get back, no doubt to face more of the music he so dreaded.

'You go on, down, Josh. I'll just say goodbye to Clueless and let myself out.'

Ben flung himself on the ever-adoring Clueless and gave him a massive hug. The dog wagged his tail and licked Ben's face, with abandoned adoration.

'You're so lucky, being a dog. You don't have to put up with any of this!'

3

THE FRIEND

Cat was finding it harder than ever to scrounge any food. The Town, while bewildering and exciting in turn, was proving to be ungenerous to a small homeless feline. Part of it was Cat's own fault, as she kept herself well hidden and ran if anyone tried to come near her, feeling quite unable to trust people. You just never knew what they might do.

Her early luck in discovering the abandoned burger in the midst of the rubbish was never repeated. On her third day in the Town the wind bore on it the smell of frying fish and, following her nose, she found herself at the far end of one of the cobbled alleyways off the Main Square, standing by a small shopfront with an open door. She stood across the other side of the alleyway and watched.

People stood in long queues and eventually they were rewarded with fishy-smelling parcels wrapped in paper, which they then tucked under their arms before marching off. Having waited until the queues had gone, she miaowed imploringly at the people behind the high counter, but they shouted at her to go away and clapped their hands at her. The marked unfriendliness frightened her and she backed away, but not without a cheeky hiss back at them. They needed to be told.

As Cat skittered down the alley with her tail between her legs the enticing smell of frying fish tormented her. She had been aware of it for an age and it sharpened the pains in her belly. She could think of nothing else. After some effort she managed to climb a wall behind the shop and jump down into the back yard, where she found a promising-smelling plastic sack. She wasted no time in ripping it open and watched with glee as it spilled all sorts of edible scraps across the yard. The small cat gorged herself until the smell of fish-scrap in batter started to make her feel sick. She was on the very point of leaving, when she was spotted by someone inside, who put up the alarm. Numerous voices started shouting – all of them at her.

'Cat! It's a cat! Get it out! Just look at that mess!' Cat tried to hide behind the bin bag, but the back door opened and to her utter horror someone flung a bucket of cold greasy water at her, soaking her long fur. She started a frantic scrabbling up the wall and she managed, with an energy fuelled by fear, to climb up and over and race away to lick herself clean again. The episode took its toll. She would never raid for fish from that shop again.

Although there had been only small showers of snow since the heavy fall four nights ago, the frost penetrated everything. Even down in the very centre of the Town, where the Main Square lay protected by its surrounding barricade of terraced houses, nothing escaped the icy grip of the cold weather and its frosty fingerprints glistened cruelly on the metal surfaces of the little drinking fountain that stood proudly in the centre of the square. The frost had turned the water solid wherever it had touched, both at the fountain's top and even below, in the deep trough at ground level.

Cat had tried licking the ice, but it had hurt her tongue and didn't at all satisfy her thirst. Each day, first thing, she would climb out of her garage and trot up her cobbled side street making straight for the Main Square where, she discovered, someone would come to replenish the peanut feeder and, Cat noticed, the same person usually broke up the ice in the drinking trough. Cat – not knowing that this was done for the sake of passing dogs and not for little cats – came to much appreciate it and would keep her eye out for the ice-breaker. She would bide her time and at the right moment, when no person was in sight to shout at her, would step forward to lap her fill. As long as she kept her thirst slaked she didn't feel her hunger so cruelly.

On her fifth day in the Town there was much disruption as big noisy lorries came round and men dumped small fir trees on their sides in great piles at every street corner. Next, more lorries with hoists on the back of them came to the Main Square. Cat watched from under a bench and saw men lifted up high to swing the trees on to the upper floor of every terraced house and shop in the square and neighbouring streets. This was followed by the arrival of a very long lorry with lots of wheels carrying an enormous tree on its back and there was even more shouting and banging and walloping than usual in the Main Square. Cat moved away. The noise was simply too much. When she returned at dusk there was a giant tree standing in the square garlanded with coloured lights and held upright by great, thick, iron wires and high up, almost out of Cat's vision, there were lines of little trees sticking out at the same angle from the second storey of every shop, also bedecked with coloured lights. It was very busy too, with lots of cars and people coming and going.

Despite the things happening in the Town, the little cat felt an overriding sense of loneliness. She had learned to keep herself discreetly in the background, remaining alone and ignored. Cat no longer trusted people. The nights seemed endlessly long and she slept fitfully as the cold seeped into her bones, but, above all, the gnawing pain in her belly kept her awake. She had attempted to raid the tortoiseshell cat's food in spite of her fear of being caught, but for the last two days the dish had been empty by the time she had arrived and as her hunger intensified, her courage diminished. She felt less able to take on a fight with another cat. Feline warriors were no more welcome than the unfriendly people who fed them.

Today, however, was a new dawn. As the cat woke and stretched her body into its most elongated form, the air around her definitely felt warmer and as she went out to meet the day she saw, with special feline appreciation, that it was sunny and clear.

As usual, Cat headed straight for the Main Square where she occupied herself by catnapping, which involved keeping one eye on the birds, of course. The snow still lay all around in dirty heaps, but larger patches of clear pavement were emerging in the thin heat of the morning sun. She had toyed with, and then abandoned, a gnawed steak bone that she had found near a bin. There had been precious little on it to eat and it reeked of dog.

In spite of her apparent languor, Cat's ears revolved to collect every sound and her nose twitched to pick up any scent of possible food or predator. It was the time of day when sometimes there would be a lull in the bustle of traffic and people. She lay in a quiet spot by a wall under a tree. As she sat hidden by the trunk of the tree, she became aware of a plump pigeon pecking around by one of the bins and she knew that this was the moment she had been waiting for.

For the whole of her life, until now, she had either suckled her mother's milk or been given solid food by her human carers and had never once had to think about where it came from. Since her arrival in the Town she had been forced to live as a scavenger, but it was against her nature. Cat might not have realised it, but she was a predator from the tip of her pert little nose to the end of her magnificent great tail. Every single thing about the way she was made combined together to make her a perfect killing machine. She had been born a hunter and, although she had never yet made use of that instinct, today the hunt was on. Enough of scavenging.

Belly low to the ground, Cat stalked forward. Her progress was painstakingly slow, so that it seemed she was barely moving at all. Every muscle was tensed, ready for movement in any direction. The pigeon had his back to her and was making stabbing pecks at the pavement, harvesting invisible morsels. As the pigeon moved, he cooed a deep throbbing 'coo roo-c'too-coo' over and again, and his head nodded up and down in time with his feet as if head and feet were connected by invisible strings. These rapid nods made the vivid greens and blues and purples of his feathers shimmer in the sunlight.

By stealth of movement, Cat was now only the length of her body away from the pigeon when he turned and saw her. She caught one glimpse of the orange bead of his eye and, tensing her muscles for full action, Cat sprang. At the same moment the pigeon fluttered his wings and started to take off and Cat, seeing this, twisted in mid-air and felled him to the ground with her extended front legs. As she landed on top of him she pinioned him to the ground by closing her jaws around his neck. The bird went limp, but Cat was taking no chances and finished it by giving him the killing bite to break his neck. He died immediately. With ravenous eagerness she turned the pigeon over and started to devour the meat from its breast. She ate as she had never eaten in her life, ignoring feathers and ripping the flesh in one great mouthful after another, crunching through bones. As her belly at last began to feel full, she spent more time plucking the feathers out with her teeth. Feathers were going everywhere and starting to blow around in the breeze.

Suddenly there was a yell. A woman rushed across the square from Cat and pushed her hard with her boot, shoving her off the bird. Cat moved to one side, but growled at the woman in a low and threatening way. Ignoring Cat, the woman bent down and picked up what remained of the pigeon. Cat slunk under a nearby bench to avoid further abuse. As she watched a man joined the woman.

'What's going on?' he said. The woman turned the carcass over in her hands, holding it up in its gory glory.

'Look at this – what a sad end!' She glared at Cat through the slats in the bench. 'I can't stand cats. Pure evil, they are.'

Cat, unaware of her so-called evilness, but having satisfied her very real need to eat, could have moved off, but a lingering feeling of ownership of her first kill held her back. The man took the pigeon's body from the woman and walked towards a litter bin across the square. Cat watched from under her bench and much later that night, when all was quiet and dark – when even the lights on the fir trees had been extinguished – she came back.

She jumped up on to the arm of the bench next to the bin and sniffed. The carcass was still there and no one else had yet found it. Cat tried to balance on the top of the bin and hook out her pigeon with a front paw, but she couldn't fish down nearly far enough. She was concerned – if she crawled through the opening she might get stuck inside. After trial and error she found she could squeeze herself through the slot and down into the depths of the bin. She quickly found her pigeon and crawled back out with bird in mouth. This time she took him back to her garage simply for the peace and quiet of it. When she got into the garage she hastily finished off the remains. Killing the pigeon had been a thing well done.

For the first time in days, Cat was no longer hungry, but she remained uneasy. She'd had quite enough of people. Unlike the ones she had known in her past life, these strangers simply couldn't be trusted. They shut you in vans, they shouted at you, they poured cold greasy water over you, they kicked you. In short they really didn't like you and some of them wanted to hurt you. Being on the run constantly from malign people, noisy traffic, smelly dogs and territorial cats, never knowing where or when she was next going to eat was utterly exhausting. Although here, in her garage, she was free to come and go, she also felt trapped and unhappy. She was beginning to grow unsure of herself.

In her old home she had felt cared for and wanted. In those days it had never occurred to her that there was any other way of being. Whenever she had wanted it there had been a cozy lap on offer, or a warm hearth to lie by, and food and water had always been available. Now, in this strange new place it took every ounce of her energy and courage just to survive. She was sad and frightened – and she was lonely.

The following morning Cat stayed in the garage until late, but eventually boredom drove her out. The sun had melted the majority of the snow and everything was wet and glistening. She passed through the Main Square, but it was market day meaning no prospect for a hunting cat. Vehicles were parked everywhere and people rushed in all directions making a great deal of noise. To get herself away from the clamour and fuss of it all, Cat sauntered around the quieter back streets and had a look for the tortoiseshell cat's food. The plate was empty.

She turned down another cobbled alley and saw some boys messing about and laughing by the back entrances of some shops. They were furtive and Cat recognised the acrid scent of struck matches. She kept close to the walls of the buildings so she wouldn't be noticed, and had almost passed by when there was an enormous bang and sparks and coloured flame shot all round her. Shrieks of laughter from the boys at the effect of their antics echoed down the road, followed by the stuttered explosions of a jumping firecracker, whose final outrage was to spin at high speed behind the terrified cat and then leap in the air before landing in front of her and continuing to jump forward.

Cat was terrified. The noise physically hurt her ears. Danger seemed to be in front of her and behind her at the same time. Her eyes opened wide, her whiskers wilted and her tail looped in stark terror between her legs and she ran so fast her heart felt as if it would burst. She tore down one long cobbled street, round a corner and across a small square she hadn't seen before. She slowed now, her heart still pounding, and followed in the lee of an immensely high wall. The wall was so tall there was no chance of her being able to get over it. A further explosion erupted from the street she had just left and she darted on again. Panic and fear gripped the little cat. She felt helpless and alone. What Cat wanted more than anything else was to crawl into a deep safe hole and sleep until all this madness was over. Her thoughts were tumbling all over each other. She had no idea whether she was being chased. It felt as if she was. Was this exploding thing like fire or did it bite? Would it hurt?

Cat reached the corner of the wall, and slowed to a walk, turning around it cautiously. She found herself face to face with a small grey squirrel who, oblivious to the commotion in the neighbouring streets, was sitting up on his hindlegs close to the base of a tall tree, gripping a pine kernel in his paws. As the cat came into view he stuffed the kernel into his mouth and chewed rapidly.

Cat looked at the squirrel and the squirrel looked back at the cat. Cat lifted her great tail, partly in surprise and partly to show her superiority to this small nut-eating rodent with sparkling eyes and twitchy whiskers. The squirrel chittered noisily at her and waved his own, not inconsiderable, tail up and down and from side to side in retaliation. He didn't seem to like being stared at. The cat didn't move a muscle as she watched the squirrel attentively. It was oddly comforting to see an equally vulnerable animal completely calm in spite of the bangs and explosions that had surrounded them. With a final dramatic wave of his great tail, the squirrel turned round and scampered up the pine tree.

Cat watched him and then felt an overwhelming desire to follow him. Too tired to hunt or to kill, Cat was simply curious. She scrambled up after the squirrel, losing sight of him in the upper branches. She arrived at a large, flat fork halfway up the tree and here she rested, giving up all hope of following the squirrel further. Cat had never been so high up a tree before. Slowly, as her heart stopped pounding, she looked around her and realised, as she relaxed, that the explosions had completely stopped and as she looked down, from high in her tree, she saw something the like of which she could never have dreamed.

Below, spread out before her, was a secret haven. The squirrel, her new friend, had led her to a refuge. A truly safe place. She let out a tiny mewl of excitement that something so beguiling could be within her reach. She was looking at a huge tree-lined garden hidden within high walls, those same walls that she had been following when she ran in her panic. Now, from this viewpoint, they appeared to be secure and cut-off from anything to do with the town.

Slowly, and with great care, she started to back down the trunk of the tree, but she found it extremely difficult. Her claws wouldn't work in reverse! Each claw hooked into the bark, but her weight then held her fast and it was difficult – almost impossible! – to lever her foot away from the tree. She reached a lower branch and stayed there for a while. Again she tried to back down, but it was too hard so, with her heart in her mouth, she turned and, going head first, she belted down the trunk until she half fell, half jumped on to the top of the wall, where she could finally stop and rest. From there it was simple to jump straight down into the garden until she was safe at last.

The garden needed to be explored with great interest and extreme thoroughness. Cat sniffed and tasted and rolled and rubbed at every point she was able. There wasn't a flowerpot, ornament, jutting wall or ancient tombstone that escaped some form of marking or examination by the little cat. At the end of her investigation Cat at last made up her mind that this garden might really be the sanctuary of peace it had promised to be from on high. The sun of the last two days had finally melted the snow and everything felt warmer. There was a distant hum of traffic from the town, but the high walls made it seem friendly and kind and safe. She could be happy here. Her only reservation was that there was a large iron gate around which – and going in all directions – she could smell the traces of many people and dogs.

Now for the buildings. They lay at one end of the enormous garden. At the side of the biggest building she spied an old, thick, wooden door slightly ajar and peeping round it to smell for danger, she crept inside.

The first thing Cat noticed was the cool stone floor beneath her paws. Her whiskers sensed the vast space above before she even looked up to the high roof, barely visible in the darkness of the building. As she padded forward she felt heat emanating from the radiators. Cat gave an involuntary shiver of pleasure and paused to do a rocking stretch, front legs and shoulders up and down and then the same with her back half, followed by a enormous yawn of satisfaction. It was the first real warmth she had felt in many days and she was enjoying every minute of it.

There was a spicy smell hanging in the air, but no scent of food. As Cat reached the end of a row of benches she turned and saw a wide area open up in front of her. A great walkway with rows of benches on either side led her eye up to the front of the building.

Cat sat down and had a good scratch while she contemplated her surroundings. She felt at ease in this place, it had an atmosphere of calm and quiet. On the far wall, close to three brightly patterned glass windows, she could see a red jar with a flame flickering in it. It interested her, so she started the long walk up the central aisle. As she drew closer, the flickering light disappeared from her vision, obscured by a high platform covered by a thick soft covering that looked as if it would be warm and cosy to lie on. As she reached the steps in front of the platform she stopped and looked around her. The sun was pouring through a side window and the front bench was drenched in a pool of warm sunlight. Cat could see motes of dust dancing wildly in the beams. She twitched her nose. The dust was lightly perfumed. Cat had been intending to spring lightly up on to the soft cloth on the altar before her, but at the last minute she changed her mind and instead hopped on to the wooden bench and settled herself on the seat, where, turning once, she curled up in a ball in the sunlight for a little snooze.

A little while later a small door opened to the right of the bench. Cat became aware of soft footsteps. Her ears flicked back and forth and she tensed as her nostrils dilated, picking up the scent of man. Cat was braced for trouble, but when the man spoke to her, his voice was low and musical and there was a gentleness in it. She opened her mouth. She had been going to make a warning hiss, but at the last minute she caught his eye and instead very quietly miaowed back at him. The man laughed and she liked the sound of it.

Gently, as if waiting for her permission, he stroked her with long cool fingers under her chin and by her ear. Cat bent her head allowing him do it. It was the first time she had received kindness in any form since she had come to this town. The man moved his hand away and Cat drew back. She felt nervous again and unsure whether she could entirely trust him.

He stood up and, turning, he walked back towards the side door. Cat watched him go and – very slowly – she followed. At first she walked hesitantly, but soon her confidence grew. Her plumed tail wafted over her back proudly, like a banner, as she trotted after him. The man turned to see if she was coming and held the door open, smiling down at her as she caught up with him and they disappeared together, into his house.

4

THE CHURCH

Ben arrived at Josh's house in a great flurry, red in the face and panting for breath. As Josh's mother opened the door she tipped her head first on one side, then on the other, trying to make eye contact with the boy in front of her. At this precise moment Ben was bent over at the waist grimacing as he clutched at the stitch in his side. When he looked up, Mrs White had cupped her hand over her nose and mouth and Ben had the strangest feeling that she was trying not to laugh.

'Now then, Ben! Where's the fire at, eh?' she said. Ben straightened up, feeling slightly foolish, and explained a little stiffly that he had come round to see if he could go out with Josh and Clueless.

The fact was that these days Ben could hardly bear to be

under the same roof as his Mum. The tension between them had been going on for days and it had come to a head this morning when Mum had finally admitted to him that his virtual dog Shadow had been officially "deleted" by the website on her orders. He had known that the account was cancelled, but actually obliterating Shadow was like having him put down: utterly final. He would never be able to get him back.

Ben had gone to his room, slamming his door so hard all the windows rattled, and flung himself on his bed where he pummelled his pillow in a blind rage, after which he had played the thumpiest, most "obnoxious" – *her* stupid word – music he could find, and it had been a minor triumph when Mum finally told him to get out from under her feet "and find something useful to do!". So in a way he was here officially, not that he told any of this to Mrs White, but she must have seen he wasn't in a jokey mood as she straightened her face.

'I'm afraid you've missed all of them. Josh went off to help Chloe take some vases down to the church. He took Clueless with him and I presume he was going to walk him somewhere afterwards. If you pop into the church you might catch them.'

Ben walked round to the church with a lot less enthusiasm in his step than when he had run to Josh's house. He knew Chloe spent a lot of time helping out here, which he'd always thought was a bit weird, but it usually meant he got to see more of Josh on his own.

Church wasn't exactly Ben's favourite thing. Going inside them made him feel awkward and this one was Catholic, which was even worse. He remembered Chloe once having a fit of giggles with him and Josh because she had been teased by a

40

schoolmate about going to a church "stuffed full of smells and bells and candles and God locked up in a box," and now Ben wondered what he was letting himself in for. He supposed he probably believed in God, but that was as far as it went.

He edged in through a side door, which he reckoned made it unofficial. But once inside the church seemed to swallow him up with its echoey enormousness. He shivered, although it wasn't really cold. The dark corners with their lurking shadows and the lightly perfumed musty smell were both strange and yet familiar. There was no sign of Josh or Chloe, or even the vases that Mrs White had mentioned. It appeared to be completely empty, with nothing at all going on. As Ben sat down in one of the long wooden pews to wait, he felt almost swamped by the quietness around him. He leaned forward to watch the light of the candle in the red jar up at the holy end. Although the candle was a long way off, its flickering was oddly calming. Ben tipped his head back slightly and squinted through his lashes at the single red light and saw multiple tiny lights twinkling back at him. The longer he sat, the more the peace of this place entered into him.

He heard the door behind him open and he turned round to see if it was Josh or Chloe, but it was a woman he didn't know. He turned back and heard her clip-clopping past him up the tiled aisle towards the altar and the red jar. She looked like she was on a mission.

Reaching the altar steps, she dropped her right knee to the floor in a deep curtsey, apparently to the candle in the jar. She stood again quickly and walked across to a very low desk with a padded step beneath it. The desk was placed in front of a statue of Mary holding the infant Jesus and the woman kneeled down on the padded step and made the sign of the cross with her right hand before leaning forward with hands clasped. Her lips moved saying silent private words.

After a while the woman stopped praying and started groping about inside her handbag. Ben leaned forward and saw her drop some coins in a little slot before she bent down to pick up one of the tea-light candles from a stack on the floor and place it on a tray in front of the statue. She lit it from the flame of one of the other candles already alight on the tray. The woman stayed motionless kneeling at her prayer desk, her face and chin illuminated by the cluster of candles lit by others who had prayed there before her. After a couple of minutes she made the sign of the cross again and walked back to where the red jar was hanging on the wall and curtseyed deep and low again. Ben realised there was an ornate casket with a gold-embossed door fixed to the wall very close to the candle in the red jar – he suddenly thought she might in fact be curtseying to the casket, not the candle. Was that what Chloe had meant when she had talked about God in a box?

As the woman turned to walk back down the aisle Ben bent his head as if in prayer, embarrassed that he had been watching her. All he could hear was the clopping of her shoes until, at last, she let herself out through the creaking main door, her mission accomplished.

The peace of the hushed building seemed to wrap itself around him comfortingly, like a warm blanket and Ben settled back on his pew, feeling at ease for the first time on this horrible day. At ease, that is, until the voices started. To begin with it was just a quiet sort of niggling that he tried to ignore, but then, slowly, the voices – or voice, one that sounded a bit like his own, kept up a non-stop jabbering, nagging away in his mind saying all sorts of cross and unkind and negative things.

The person who was the focus of all this pent-up fury was his mother. It was all her fault. Everything. It was *she* who was to blame. She had made him do it. Never listening to him, never giving him any money. All she did was go on and on. Nothing he did was ever right. And, oh, how she made heavy weather of everything, absolutely *everything*! As he thought about the things she'd said and what she'd done as punishment he ached with anger.

No computer, no email and worst of all no Shadow. Ben missed that dog more than he could easily explain to anyone. It was like a raw wound. It was like losing part of himself. When his mother had finally revealed that she had requested that his cyberdog should be deleted, her face had been all twisted up in a strange way. With triumph – that was it! Ben was sure of it. As Ben relived her words he thought again about that word *deleted*. Her final, total, absolute, mean, vile, selfish punishment.

The boy kicked out at the pew in front of him and slumped forward to lean on it. Burying his head in his arms, he sobbed. Deep, racking tears of stifled grief shook his whole body. Never in his life had he felt such a turmoil of emotions. As he drew a deep breath between sobs, he became aware of footsteps drawing close to the end of his pew. He stopped. He stopped *everything*, including breathing.

Looking down – he was far too embarrassed to look up – Ben saw a large pair of men's shoes peeping out from under what looked like a long black dress. Whoever it was, was standing really close and must have heard the awful noises Ben had been making. Ben breathed out at last and, reluctantly, he let his eyes travel slowly up the figure towering above him. Without realising he was doing it Ben found himself starting to count the astonishing number of buttons that ran the full length of the robe, until he finally reached the face of the man wearing this strange attire. Ben registered the white dog-collar and the beginning of a lop-sided smile beneath a pair of gentle, questioning brown eyes. As with all people in uniform the man's age was hard to guess, but Ben reckoned he was quite a bit younger than Mum.

'You know what they say, better out than in,' the man said. The lop-sided smile had now grown into a broad grin. But then, slowly, the man's face grew serious. 'You might feel better if you share whatever it is that's hurting you that much. It doesn't have to be with me. But here, in this house of God, is a good place to unload. I'll listen or, if you prefer, just God can listen.' There was a pause. Then he spoke again. 'I've always found God to be a right good listener.'

Ben's eyes widened in surprise on hearing the northern twang – he had always thought priests were a bit posh. The man seated himself in the pew in front of Ben, his head tilted as if he was waiting for Ben to speak out. And Ben found he did want to talk – and talk he did.

When Ben first started it all came out in rush and he got all muddled up and wasn't sure what it was that he wanted to say.

The words tumbled out over each other and he had to keep going back to the beginning again.

The priest held up his arms as if in I surrender.

'Now then, lad – just you take your time. Only tell me what you want and whatever you tell me will go no further. But let's introduce ourselves. My name's Father John-Henry Monk and I'm priest of this parish – most folk round here call me Father John-Henry. Now, it's your turn to tell me what your name is and, hey lad, while you're at it, don't forget to breathe!'

The boy grinned and, as instructed, took a deep breath. Slowly he explained who he was and then as he gathered momentum he started to unload all the grief and anger that was fizzing inside him. Soon Ben found himself telling Father John-Henry how it seemed nothing he ever did was enough for Mum, that everything – even his dad leaving – seemed to be his fault. At this point Ben chewed at his bottom lip.

'And it's true – he never bothers to come and see us any more. But he went off with that Tracy and I would have thought *she* must be something to do with it?' Ben looked at the priest to see if he agreed, but he just nodded his head, waiting for the boy to talk on. 'Now, with this latest stuff, I just don't believe how she could—'

'Hold on, Ben. You're losing me here. What stuff?'

'My cyberdog, Shadow – he was my mate, my pal. Mum's just been so out of order. So unfair and . . . and . . . yes – cruel. Really cruel. I mean what she's done . . . her punishment, I suppose. She's deleted him. She's killed Shadow! Killed him!' Ben stopped. He was worried he might cry. Father John-Henry leaned forward.

'Ben, can you explain to me why your mum would want to punish you?'

Ben stared back at the priest silently and shrugged, wearing an expression of bewildered innocence.

'Ben, your mum wouldn't just "kill" your dog, your what do you call it, your cyberdog, for no reason. Come on, start at the beginning and –' Father John-Henry looked puzzled, '– while you're at it could you explain what a cyberdog is?'

Ben frowned, wondering what the beginning was.

'I've always wanted a dog.' Yes, that was definitely the start. 'Always, from when I was really little. And I asked Mum and Dad loads of times – every birthday and Christmas and sometimes in between – for a dog and they always said no.' Ben pulled his forlorn face. But then he looked up and grinned. 'And then I found this website, well my friend Josh, you know Josh – and his sister Chloe – he told me about it. You become a member and then you get a cyberpet and you give him a personality. You sort of create him. And I created this wonderful dog called Shadow and he was loyal and faithful and he loved me. When I was online with Shadow anything was possible, absolutely anything and it felt so good.' Ben rocked back and forth thinking about Shadow. 'And I bought him loads of things, like toys and stuff. The more stuff you buy for the pets, the more things you can make them do. And it got so as I could imagine him up even when I wasn't near the computer, but now he's been destroyed I can't seem to picture him any more.'

As he said this last sentence Ben's voice went low with despair and his eyes filled with tears. He fell silent for several long moments.

'You're really angry with your mother aren't you? Why?' Father John-Henry asked.

'I've explained it,' Ben said. His voice was harsh. 'She killed my dog and it looked like she enjoyed it, too.'

'What makes you say she enjoyed it, Ben?'

Ben screwed up his face in frustration and had a long think. 'Because of the look on her face when she told me,' he said. 'It felt almost, gleeful or something. Her mouth was all funny and twisted. Like she was triumphant in some way!'

'But Ben, *why* did your mother destroy Shadow?'

Ben remained silent.

'Was it punishment for something?'

'Um, well, I used her credit card to get a year's subscription and premier membership – it meant I could buy all the stuff. It was easier to do it all in one go.'

'How did you manage that?'

'I borrowed her card – without her knowing – and entered all the details and that.'

'I suppose that it came to quite a lot of money, did it?'

'Sixty nine, ninety nine,' said Ben quietly.

'Ben have you tried, at any point, to imagine what it might have felt like to be your mother when she discovered what you had done?' As he said this the priest looked at Ben intently.

Ben shook his head in silence. The priest lowered his gaze. After a pause he cleared his throat and started to speak again.

'Do you know what you did that really upset her?'

Ben flexed his shoulder blades together, discomfited, and put his head down. 'I s'pose it was the credit card fraud,' he mumbled.

'Ben – you call it "credit card fraud". Try giving it another name.'

Ben kept his head down. A long aching minute ticked by and the boy looked up to find the eyes of the priest upon him, but his face was gentle, not stern. Ben grimaced and took a deep breath.

'I s'pose you could call it stealing?'

'Ben, you have to decide yourself what *you* call it.'

Another long pause. 'It was stealing.' One large tear rolled down his cheek and plopped on to the back of his hand. He shook it off violently as if doing so meant it hadn't happened. No tear. No upset. No crime. But more tears followed.

'How do you think your mother feels?'

'Don't know.' Ben pushed his shoe up and down the back of the pew in front so it squeaked. 'Cross?'

'Anything else?' the priest asked.

'Upset? Depressed?'

'Do you think she could be disappointed in you?'

'Probably! She often is!' Ben pulled his sleeve across his nose and sniffed noisily. The priest stood up.

'I know this much, Ben, however much she might be hurt by all of this, she will still love you.' Father John-Henry turned to smile down at Ben kindly.

Ben frowned. 'How do you know? You've never met her, have you?'

'No, but I know that's what a mother's love is like.' The priest sat down again and looked deep into Ben's eyes. 'Ben – you need to think about whether you really believe she enjoyed telling you what she'd had to do to Shadow. And –' as he said this the priest started to stand up once more, '– you could try saying sorry, that might help?'

At that moment there was a clattering at the sacristy door and the sound of distant giggles that Ben recognised as belonging to Chloe and a look of panic flashed across his face. Father John-Henry shook his head reassuringly and told him not to worry.

'I have to go now. The church is always open . . . well, until dusk. You can always pop in for a quiet word with God.'

At that moment Chloe burst into the church carrying something in her arms and Father John-Henry nearly collided with her on his way out. Ben heard him laughing as he passed.

'Next up, Chloe, you'll be putting clothes on that cat and wheeling her about in a pram.'

Chloe giggled as the image took hold in her mind's eye. As she got closer, Ben was struck by the strong resemblance that she had to her brother, with the same wide-set eyes, freckled nose and silvery blond hair. Chloe's long hair was usually pulled back in a high ponytail, which she would toss around to indicate her moods, whereas Josh kept his hair short, except for his floppy fringe, which he constantly flipped out of his eyes.

'Wayhay, Ben. Fancy seeing you here – look what I've got!'

Ben could now see she was cradling a loudly protesting cat on its back, like a human baby. He was astonished that a cat was allowed in a church, but he just gave a feeble grin. The cat was thrashing her fluffy tail crossly back and forth and, as Ben watched, the cat had clearly had enough. She wriggled herself upright and leaped in a giant arc, landing with feather-like grace on the stone-flagged floor of the church. There she started a fussy grooming of herself to remove all trace of the humiliation she had suffered.

Chloe shrugged, laughing, and flopped down beside Ben explaining eagerly that Father John-Henry had officially rescued the cat – although in fact the cat had found him. She said that they all reckoned the poor thing had endured a pretty tough time and now the priority was to try to get some weight on her.

'She's still horribly thin, but she'll get better soon. We reckon she must've had a home – although she's really jumpy, she's still very different from those feral cats that just run a mile. And hey, isn't he brill?'

'When you say "isn't he brill" are you talking about the cat or your priest?' Ben asked, somewhat unnecessarily, as it was perfectly obvious who Chloe was talking about. Besides, Chloe'd already said the cat was a she, not a he – not that Ben would've known the difference.

'Father John-Henry, of course. What were the two of you talking about?'

'Just things.'

'Was it helpful?'

Ben went silent. He wasn't sure whether it had been or not. What he did know was that he didn't really want to talk about it. He pulled his brows together and frowned.

'The question wasn't that difficult. Did he sort you out?' Chloe insisted.

'Sort of, but . . . I wasn't sure whose side he was on.' Ben looked up and down the church, desperate to change the subject and feeling worried that Chloe might ask him more questions. 'Is Josh around? There's something I need to ask him.' He stood up and pulled up his anorak zip as if was about to depart.

Chloe laughed and said Josh couldn't get out of church fast enough. As soon as he had dumped the vases he went off with Clueless to meet up with a couple of other boys and their dogs at the rec. for a kick about. Ben listened with a sinking heart. That would mean he couldn't crash in and join them – being dog-less he would only be in the way.

Ben turned away, trying to hide his crestfallen face, but Chloe touched his arm. He looked back at her to see what she wanted and to his surprise she just wrinkled her nose at him. With an impish toss of her head, she announced firmly that she'd done quite enough good works for one Saturday and she was off.

After the outer door closed Ben sat down on a pew near the back of the church. Following Chloe's lively presence the church seemed strangely quiet. He slumped down wearily, but now he was on his own he had a chance to think more about his conversation with Father John-Henry. He had a strong feeling that after all that talking he ought to *do* something, but he wasn't sure what and the more he thought about it the more he felt embarrassed about the whole thing. Unless . . . perhaps if he said sorry, here, in the church, it would make things better?

A bit uncertainly, Ben rose and walked round the back of the pews, passing the cat who, leg high in the air mid-groom, simply ignored him. Ben looked at the cat and wondered if Clueless would be allowed in here, but decided probably not. So it seemed it was different rules for cats then? Why, he wondered, were cats considered different?

Ben turned to walk up to the altar, glancing as he got there to check he was alone. Seeing the candle in its red jar next to the gold casket he self-consciously bowed his head in a nod to God, then looked to the side at the cheerful shelf of candles beneath the statue of Mary. Going over, Ben dug in his pocket and all he could find was a five pence piece. He wondered if it was too small to offer as payment for a candle, but finding no instructions he shrugged and popped it into the slot for coins. Ben took a fresh candle and lighting it from one of the others he placed it on the tray. He held up his palms to the tiny wavering flames as if warming his hands by a fire and then, worried he might be seen, he stepped back. As he watched the flickering candle he half closed his eyes and slowly and silently he mouthed one word.

'*Sorry.*'

As Ben walked back down the aisle, a curious sense of relief lightened his step and as he passed the cat he bent down and gently touched her back with two fingers.

The effect was electric. Ben stood still. He could barely breathe. The cat stopped her grooming and looked up at Ben with shining golden eyes. She had felt it too.

5

THE CAT

The instant his fingers touched her back, Cat knew. The boy was someone she could love like no one else she had ever met. The little cat studied Ben intensely. Her animal instinct told her that this boy should become a significant part of her life – she needed to know everything there was for a cat to know about a boy. She watched him hesitate, uncertain, before he slid into one of the pews. He kept glancing over, watching her. Normally that would have made her uncomfortable, but now it intrigued her. She was excited.

Cat needed to get a real sense of him up close. She jumped on to the pew in front of him and, with an exquisite sense of balance, she inched her way along until her eyes were level with his. She breathed in his scent and it filled her with happiness. As she looked up, she tipped her head towards him enquiringly. Her eyes were big and full of compassion. She saw his surprise and sensed his interest, but she also had a feeling he was holding back. Cat would just have to move in closer still. She edged forward and gently headbutted the hand that rested on her pew. When he inhaled, she looked up to find him watching her and she returned his gaze, making a long, nearly silent, miaow to him – a whispered greeting, meant for him alone. The boy grinned broadly and Cat relaxed.

Jumping on to the seat next to him she slowly, shyly, crept on to his knee. She felt the warmth of his body through his clothes and, after kneading him with her feet, she turned about and settled herself into a round ball on his lap. A perfect fit.

At first the boy's hand fluttered uncertainly over her head and body. He was almost, but not quite, stroking her. And then, slowly, Cat felt his other hand encircle her and hold her more firmly. Cat turned her head and licked his fingers with her rough tongue. The boy's tension had been like a physical barrier stopping her getting through to him, but now he relaxed and stroked her with supreme gentleness. She could sense the very essence of this boy from his smell and the way he held her. She liked his smell. The small cat felt a wave of contentment pass over her. Her gladness poured out of her in a gentle purr. Enjoying the sensation it gave her, she wanted to share it with this special boy and she purred louder until her body thrummed with the power of it. Ben's hands clasped her more surely . . .

The church door banged loudly. Ben let go of the cat in surprise and leaping to his feet he turned around. Cat, losing her lap so abruptly, jumped to the ground and started grooming in order to compose herself. They both looked across in the direction of the offending door, but there was no one there, it was only the wind.

Ben, rather fussily, started to brush away her long hairs from his trousers mumbling that he might just wander up to the rec. after all and have some fun with the dogs.

'There's tons of things you can do with a dog, you know.'

Cat made no comment. Her mind was on other matters. She wanted to be let out into the garden, and, since she could see that Ben was going to go out of the wrong door, she went to stand by the small side door and miaowed at him to assist her. He understood and, with a grin and a mock bow, he did as he was asked.

Cat stood at the head of the path that ran the length of the walled garden and heard the far door slam shut as Ben left. As the cool December breeze reached Cat's nostrils her nose twitched. Patiently, she unravelled the scents of all the comings and goings that had taken place recently within the walled garden. No enemy that she could recognise had come a-calling so, floating her great tail high in the air and with a confident shimmy of her hips, she sauntered down the ancient flagged path in search of whatever the day might have to offer.

Finding this garden, had been the very best thing that had happened to her since she had left her last home. Living here with the priest felt safe. Cat sensed he would never hurt her or shout at her. After the unexpected hostility she had experienced from the townsfolk, her trust in people was returning to her only slowly and Father John-Henry was helping her greatly to find faith in humans again.

Indeed, life here was good; Cat was kept warm and comfortable at all times and the meals came regularly. One of the things that Cat enjoyed about Father John-Henry was that he talked to her as he pottered around the house, in a quiet and companionable way that made her remember how human friendship was something she had taken for granted in the past. It would be some time before she would assume all humans would behave like that, but for now Cat enjoyed her new home and her kindly priest. Another human with whom she had formed a tentative bond was Chloe, who had become a favourite of the little cat, as she always went out of her way to play. Cat had missed that kind of fun while she had been living rough. She could even tolerate, for a short time, Chloe carrying her around on her back in return for the playtimes they shared.

But Ben was altogether different. Once Cat had properly taken him in she had felt a magnetic attraction towards him, one which had been amplified the moment he stroked her back. The little cat knew she could heal the hurt she could feel in him by loving him and giving him her courage. Hidden within the boy there was a peace, which – if he would allow it – she could set free. Cat felt in Ben a quite special tenderness. Father John-Henry was gentle but Ben, she could tell, was on her wavelength. At the moment Ben didn't trust her or understand her, but that could change – *Cat* could change that.

As Cat continued patrolling her new territory she turned her mind to the walled garden and what pleasures it might hold. Although it was December the sudden rise in temperature was being enjoyed by the native birds who, now that the ice and snow had disappeared, were feeding themselves with wild abandon. The air was throbbing with interesting sounds and filled with scents that made Cat's mouth water. Her need to hunt in order to eat had ceased since she had been reintroduced to the comforts of home living, but her curiosity about the wildlife around her remained as sharp as ever.

As she walked in the lee of the wall, the warning churring of the dominant cock blackbird irritated her ears. His repetitive alarm call alerting his mate and all others to the presence of a prowler was unnecessarily loud and made it much harder to hear the other winter wildlife. She chittered her teeth crossly to herself as her ears flicked back and forth. Above the blackbird's harsh warnings, she could hear the repeated calls of one chaffinch to another as they hopped around the undergrowth. They were well camouflaged but their strident drawn out '*prink, prink, prink, prink, prink, prink*,' cries warning each other of an encroaching enemy made it impossible for the cat to stalk them. She stood still regarding their handsome tan-and-fawn waistcoats and the white flash of the bars as they fluttered their wings. The birds flew off, just to be safe, and Cat continued her walk with implacable calm.

She turned to follow the high wall at the end of the garden, behind which she could hear the river rushing over stones and, in front of her, she heard a strangely wistful, whistling call that died away in its final notes. As she watched she saw a chubby brown bird with a startling pink breast and white rump land on a low-hanging seed feeder to one side of the path. In a few seconds he was joined by his equally dumpy, bull-necked wife in her more discreet buff livery with matching white rump, and together they swung in unison. Cat's whiskers curled forwards in interest as she watched the pair of resident bullfinches. Although she thought about a quick strike, she changed her mind at the last moment. Instead she headed for the large potting shed that housed all sorts of interesting things, and which she used as a welcome shelter whenever she got shut out of the house and church.

Cat crept round to the open window, sprang through it and softly down to the floor. Having checked that there were no unwanted visitors, she settled down in a patch of sun to groom. The long slanting rays of the winter sunlight touched her snow-white chest making her glow gold. She ceased to groom as she lifted her head to enjoy the warmth of the sun, and in so doing she spotted a creature quite unlike any she had seen before. She found herself staring at a small, highly patterned, black-and-white hunting spider – a zebra spider – moving down the wall near the window. She walked across and pushed her nose right up to him. Perhaps he would make a good snack? As she sniffed deeply, she caught a whiff of the poison contained within his fangs and quickly pulled back. Perhaps, instead, she might play with him a little?

As she watched, keeping her face well clear of those toxic fangs, she realised that the spider had lifted his head curiously and was watching her back with two enormous eyes at the front of his head. Unknown to Cat he had six further eyes, making his vision truly remarkable. The two creatures maintained their scrutiny of each other for several moments, but in the end the spider won out – more eyes – and the cat moved away. Cat continued her inspection from a short distance away, intrigued by this brightly coloured homesteader.

The spider was now concentrating on a tiny cluster fly that, warmed out of semi-hibernation by the deceitful winter sun, was bumbling clumsily around the windowpane. As soon as the spider saw potential prey his posture changed and he turned to face the fly directly. He squatted low down and started to stalk, exactly as a cat does. Almost stationary at times, he crept forward by tiny amounts until he was extremely close, yet the fly remained oblivious.

At this point Cat was surprised to see the spider make a lightning strike at the fly against the windowpane. His jump was so fast it was barely visible. As the zebra spider made contact with the fly a brief buzzing battle ensued before the fly fell silent, paralysed, then crushed, by the jaws of its killer. The spider settled down to eat, only to be disturbed when Cat stood up. The jumping spider, however, like any skilled mountaineer, had made sure his safety line was attached to his wall by the window and so he quickly returned to the wall from which he had launched himself, to watch until the coast was clear.

Cat blinked and yawned widely. Rising, she stretched out, long and lean; now her front half and then her back half, shaking each leg in turn. She licked her lips. It was time to return to the house in search of the proper cat food she knew would be hers. All she had to do was to ask and it would be given.

As Cat walked into the kitchen, she '*prrrpd*' a brief greeting to the priest and walked over to her empty bowl, sitting down neatly in front of it, folding her tail tidily over her toes. She looked up at the man in the long black dress and miaowed with an unmistakeable note of pleading.

Father John-Henry smiled and filled her bowl from a sachet of cat food, for which she thanked him with a long '*mnnnnneow*'. He talked to her gently in his low melodic voice as she ate and Cat enjoyed the companionship. It felt homely. After she had eaten she licked her whiskers clean of any scent of food and the priest bent down to stroke his fingers up the length of her magnificent tail, telling her how beautiful she was. Cat '*prrrrpd*' her pleasure at being stroked and then, because she was a cat, she forgot all about him and moved away a small distance to groom, so the priest left her to it.

Later, when she remembered him again, Cat found the priest in his study, talking into the phone. She jumped up on to the desk and started to play with his pen.

'Yes, and talk of the devil. This very minute she's just upped and landed on my desk. I admit it's wonderful having her here. She's grand company. But you should have seen her when she first arrived, she was just a wee scrap of a thing, all skin and bone. It was pitiful. Her coat was in knots and covered in fleas. But yup, already, she's put on a bit of weight . . . Yes, yes, that's exactly it . . . The cat. This heart surgery means I have to go into hospital immediately after Christmas and then there's the recovery. I'll be away for close on eight weeks.'

The priest pulled his hand through his hair as a voice the other end rattled into his ear. 'Oh I know all that. That's the trouble with animals, as soon as they enter your life you become responsible. But I didn't intend for it to happen, she chose me.' He laughed a deep chortle in response to the other person. 'Let me know if you have a brainwave of any kind. Meanwhile I'll put my thinking cap on!'

Father John-Henry rescued his pen from Cat's deft front paws and started to write on his pad. As he did so, she patted the writing tip gently with her paw making him laugh as he gripped the pen more firmly. The phone call came to an end and the priest returned the pen to the cat for her to play with it. As she delicately hooked it up in her protracted claws and dropped it down on the notepad, the message that had just been written could be seen very clearly:

URGENT - find a good home for the cat

Cat yawned. She had finished with the pen now that he had. She jumped from the desk and wandered across to her favourite armchair – the one with the red velvet cushion. Springing lightly up, she turned round three times and settled down for a cosy nap.

6

THE BOY

Ben sat on a bench grinning broadly. With one foot up on the seat, he had hooked his arms around his knee so it wouldn't escape and he rocked happily to and fro watching Josh hurling sticks for Clueless. The dog's eagerness to "fetch" – in *and* out of water – knew no bounds and his energy seemed inexhaustible, although his ability to predict where his stick might actually land left much to be desired. Ben loved Saturdays, well, certainly Saturdays like this. Ben was at his happiest when in the company of Josh and his dog.

Normally he and Josh talked about *things* – practical things – like what they might do, or programmes they had watched or computer games they wanted, or football or Clueless. They rarely talked about feelings. But since last Saturday, when Ben had said so much to Father John-Henry, he felt as if a great stopper had been removed and he could open his mouth and talk about anything at all. Already they'd talked about one of their teachers, Mrs Matthews, who Ben thought had got it in for him, although Josh suggested she just said things in a bossy way and what she actually said was all right.

Ben got up and stood next to Josh on the bank, so he could throw sticks as well. Both boys ended up laughing and name-calling as they tried to duck behind each other to avoid a soaking from the dog as he emerged for the umpteenth time spraying them liberally with river water.

'Why does he shake himself before he's even out of the water?' Ben gasped. 'I swear it makes him wetter.'

'Because he's Clueless, that's why,' Josh said.

'Ouch! I asked for that!' Ben rolled his eyes. 'Talking of being clueless you won't believe what Mum's gone and done!'

'Go on, try me.'

'Are you ready for this one?' Ben puffed out his cheeks just thinking about it. 'Last night she told me – like she *really* expected me to be pleased, that my main Christmas present this year was going to be a cat!'

As Ben was speaking, Clueless, whose supply of sticks seemed to have evaporated, came and sat at Ben's feet watching his face closely, putting his head first on one side and then on the other.

'What's more it's going to be a manky old second-hand cast-off from *your* church! I mean, Josh, a *cat*! Of all the things in the world they might give me – a cat, I ask you!' At the final shout of 'cat', Clueless barked loudly, lowered his front legs and, whining, wiggled his hindquarters excitedly before jumping up and barking again. Clueless liked cats! He *loved* them and even the word excited him! Josh couldn't stop himself laughing.

'Oh, bad luck mate, that's rough, that's really rough,' he said but he was still grinning his head off.

'I told her I didn't want a blimmin' cat. The awful thing is, though, that when I said I wanted a dog, I knew all along I wouldn't get one but she promised, *actually* promised they would get me a second-hand Playstation to make up for Shadow not being around any more. But this cat thing is just awful. It's like going back on everything she promised when I was really upset. Anyway she certainly knows how I feel now.' Ben was shaking from the mix of emotions he was holding in. He breathed deeply.

'Did you say you'd prefer a Playstation to a cat?' Josh asked.

'I did and the awful thing is that she never said a word. Nothing. All she did was put her head down in the palm of her hand and let out one of those huge sighs of hers, kind of like she was disappointed in me. Like I was being really difficult or something.' Ben pulled his most woeful face. 'Is it really *that* bad not to want a stupid cat?'

Josh touched his arm sympathetically. Clueless, sensing Ben's sadness, nudged his wet nose in a friendly manner straight into Ben's crotch. Ben squawked in protest, but as he held his hands out to the dog, instead of pushing him away, he held the great heavy head and looked Clueless deep in the eyes.

'All I really wanted was a dog. A big, gentle, licky dog like you that I could go out and play games with and take for walks and who would adore me. Or, second best, was Shadow who went everywhere with me. And what's happened? A cat's happened – that's what. And not even a kitten but an already grown-up second-hand stray cat!'

Ben turned back to Josh and shrugged, despairing. 'And it's all because that priest got involved. I can't believe he called my mum. He said he wouldn't tell anyone what I'd told him.' Ben flung the stick he had been holding for Clueless angrily into the water. The dog, thinking the game was over, was looking the wrong way and missed his chance so the stick was gone for ever.

'What did you tell him?' Josh asked and Ben remembered that he never did tell his friend what happened in the church.

'Oh everything. You know, the stuff about Mum and the credit card bill.' Josh went very still. Ben looked up, surprised by the long silence. Josh looked as if he was thinking hard.

'Did Father John-Henry suggest you do anything to make things better?' Josh asked eventually.

'No, he just asked loads of questions. About Mum and stuff. I think he wanted me to admit to myself that I'd done something *bad*. And . . .' Ben paused as he thought. 'And . . . I kind of did. After he and Chloe had gone I thought I might light a candle and say sorry. Sort of . . .'

Ben frowned after he had said this. He went quiet and looked down at his right shoe, which was doing a funny sort of solo jig without his having any control over it. Josh looked thoughtful and said, so quietly that Ben could hardly hear him, that he thought he'd better go and see Father John-Henry about *his* part in the whole affair as well.

'What for?' Ben asked.

'I feel bad about it. If I'd never suggested it . . .'

'I can make up my own mind about what I do, Josh. You didn't make me do anything. You don't have to apologise for me, honestly!'

'No, it would be for my own sake, not yours, you silly!' Josh added in a fond voice.

'Are you as into all that as Chloe, then?' Ben asked, but Josh explained that, although he went to church on Sundays, he didn't take the whole thing as seriously as Chloe, who, since their confirmation, practically lived round there.

'Although we're twins, we *are* separate beings and we don't always agree about everything. I feel just as close to you as I do to her. I can talk to you about things she doesn't understand.'

Ben felt the weight of doubt lift off his shoulders. Maybe Josh *was* interested in Ben's life after all? And Ben started to talk and talk and talk. First about the problems he felt at home; his mother always seeming so tired and only ever seeing the negative side of everything. Then about how he was sad too that he never saw his father. Even less often, now he'd moved away with Tracy, who (as his mother never tired of saying) was "nearly half his age". Around the town Dad had been regarded by everyone as an all-round great guy and some people even called him Cheerful-Charlie-Ainscough, as if it was one long name, always ready to tell a tall tale or a dodgy joke. And, Ben added with feeling, he was utterly fed up with being told what a comedian he had for a dad because, when it came to it, his Dad never had enough time for him. Where was the laugh in that?

'When Dad still lived with us, he used to take me to football, but it's over two years since he took me to a match.'

Josh chortled. 'Well, that's one up on me. My dad has

66

never taken me to football. Not even once. He can't stand it.'

The boys turned away from the river and started to walk home, while Clueless ran in mad circles around them, chasing the odd seagull out of pure joy.

'Why don't you talk to your mum?' Josh said. But Ben didn't have an answer to that.

Walking home from Josh's, Ben felt a sudden spasm of guilt that although he'd had plenty bad to say about the priest's cat he'd never mentioned his strangely positive encounter with the very same cat when he'd been about to leave the church – that astonishing flash of electricity between them. Embarrassed, he kicked a small stone into a spin along the pavement, then reasoned to himself that as Josh was a total dog-man he wouldn't have believed it anyway. Still, the more Ben thought back on his conversations with Josh on all the other things they talked of the more he hugged himself, feeling a wave of pleasure that came with trust. Josh's friendship meant a great deal to Ben and a shadow of insecurity that had been lurking was gone.

What Josh had said stayed with him and later that day Ben decided that he should say sorry to his mother. Saying sorry in church was one thing, but was it enough? When he thought about the twisted look on his mother's face when she told him about closing down his imaginary pet account, he realised now that she'd been upset, not triumphant. Yes, saying sorry to her was definitely the right thing to do. And then, after apologising, he would be able to persuade her that giving him a cat was a really bad idea and talk her out of it.

The thing to do was to find the right time. Evenings were

tricky, what with tea and homework and then watching telly in the front room. It was difficult to talk across the noise of the TV, although Ben was never sure Mum had been watching anyway – her cleaning jobs seemed to take it out of her and she often snoozed in her armchair.

Tonight, by chance, he was in luck. A storm had been growing in ferocity ever since he had got home and the wind, which was howling in from the north west, increased in a series of squalls. A giant gust of wind rattled crossly at the windows, puffed huffily down the chimney and whistled through a crack in the door. Then, as quickly as it had come, it crept away.

But just as everything seemed to go quiet, the electrics blew and darkness descended. No polite warning flickers to say 'Something amiss – prepare yourself,' one minute it was all cosy-yellow glow and happy-chatty stuff on telly and the next it was pitch black and quiet as the grave.

The silence was broken by Mum stumbling in from the kitchen, where she had been getting their meal ready, to see whether the whole house was without power. The red glow from the wood burner provided them with a low light as their eyes got used to the darkness. Mum opened up the stove and flung more logs on it, announcing that she would cook on it and Ben fetched the emergency candles. As he started to light them, Ben realised that the atmosphere was totally different in this shadowy jumpy light. He held his arms out wide with his fingers bentand splayed so their blown-up silhouettes leaped up the walls and along the ceiling. He made 'Whooo . . .' noises pretending to be a ghost (but sounding remarkably like their local owl). To his surprise Mum joined in, making Ben laugh.

In the unusual intimacy of this candlelit BBQ atop the stove and egged on by Mum's good mood, Ben at last found the courage to apologise.

'Mum?'

She glanced up at him and Ben screwed up his face and shut his eyes.

'Something I've wanted to say for a bit . . . I *am* sorry about what I did.'

Ben opened his eyes, but his mum had turned to fiddle with the bacon and sausages in the pan, her back to him. Perhaps she didn't know what he was talking about.

'About the credit card thing and the imaginary pet website.'

She turned and threw him a weak smile, and in the glow of the firelight he thought he glimpsed relief in her eyes. There was a long pause.

'But, Mum, do I *have* to have a cat?'

His mother's face fell. 'Oh, Ben. It's already been arranged.'

'Well, can't you un-arrange it?' Ben said quickly.

'Father John-Henry and I both think it will be good for you to have a real animal to love. You need to get over this cyberdog,' Mum said.

Ben's frustration and hurt dampened down all his good intentions towards his mother. Shadow *was* real to him – couldn't she see that?

'How come Father John-Henry came sneaking round to see you? When I talked to him in church he said it was private.' Ben slumped down at a table and squashed his face between his hands. 'Now he's telling tales and trying to get rid of his scabby cat into the bargain.'

His mother crossed the room and put her hand across his shoulders.

'Ben, love, you've got it completely wrong.' Her tone was sad but gentle. 'Father John-Henry advertised for someone to take care of his house after Christmas. He's going away for a while – it can't be helped – and that's why he has to find a home for the cat.' Ben raised his head and actually looked at his mother. 'I went to his house to talk about the job.' She caught Ben's eye and smiled at him, shyly, unconsciously tidying a stray hair back into its wayward knot. 'While I was there the cat came into the room and that's how we ended up speaking about the pair of you. He never said a word about whatever it was you said to him in the church – he just said that you had a lot of love to give and his cat would be a good place to start.'

Ben felt a wave of relief realising that Father John-Henry hadn't betrayed his trust.

'So have you got the job, then?' Ben asked.

'Yes. There's a retired priest coming to cover while Father John-Henry's away, and he's got some sort of cat allergy, which is why the cat's got to go. So when he starts he will have to approve of me and then, fingers crossed, it will be official.'

Ben was glad about the job. But he longed to say what he truly felt on the matter of the cat, only he knew it was hopeless. He remembered with sharp clarity the way he'd thought that if he said sorry to his mother everything would be all right. Well now he had – and it was . . . but the cat was coming, like it or not.

70

7

THE MAGNIFICAT

One night, during the last week of term, Ben found himself trailing down the road in Chloe's wake, balancing a borrowed cat-carrier on his head. He let out a sigh large enough to be heard by Chloe. In the ghostly glow of an orange street-light he saw Chloe look back at him with a raised eyebrow.

'You are funny, Ben. I always had you down as a lover of all animals, not just dogs, like Josh. He can't stand cats.'

'I do love all animals, but dogs are the best. They're so loving and eager to please, you can play with them and go places with them as well. Cats are different.' As Ben finished saying this the cat carrier crashed to the ground, the door dropped off and the spindle rolled into the road.

'Oh Ben, you're making awful heavy weather of carrying

that cat cage! Here, let me help you.' Chloe ran back and got him reorganised.

Ben, if asked, would have said he would prefer spending time with Josh, so he was surprised to find hanging about with Chloe was kind of fun – she was very direct and straightforward about things. On the other hand going to church and collecting a cat was not his idea of a great evening. There was no way out, he'd never wanted a cat in the first place – but this wasn't about what he wanted, so he gritted his teeth. And changed the subject.

'What's the best time to go to the dentist?' he said.

Chloe stopped and turned round, confused.

'Tooth-hurty!' Ben said quickly, before she could answer. Chloe walked back to the dawdling Ben and whacked him on the arm, laughing.

'I've got one for you. What happened to the cat that swallowed a ball of wool?' She lifted her finger to his lips and shook her head at him so he wouldn't answer back. 'She had mittens, lots and lots of them! So be warned . . .'

Ben groaned and they both giggled.

It had been dark for over two hours and as they approached the church they saw a dim glow shining through the windows, but not all the lights were on and it seemed eerily gloomy once they were inside. The choir was busy rehearsing something next to the organ, where most of the light came from. They heard the organist break off and ask individual choristers to sing certain lines again. Eventually he seemed satisfied and asked them to sing it through.

Ben dug Chloe in the ribs and asked in a whisper what they

were singing. Chloe shrugged and said it sounded like a Taizé chant to her. That didn't mean a thing to Ben.

'It's in some weird language!'

'That's Latin, you idiot, and only in bits of it,' Chloe laughed. At that moment a swell of voices rang out.

'*Magnificat, Magnificat anima mea Dominum,*' they sang.

'They're singing about a blimmin' cat!'

Chloe smiled and gave a little skip, pulling Ben after her towards the choir. As they got to the end of the aisle they saw that the side door was open and, as they looked, they saw the small, white-bibbed, golden-eyed cat walk slowly into church, her majestic tail wafting from side to side above her back. She glided in front of the altar, then, as she got to the aisle where Ben and Chloe stood, she turned and walked slowly and gracefully the full length of the church pointing out her front feet like a model on a catwalk. She passed Father John-Henry, who was standing by the choir, without so much as a glance – her eyes completely on Ben.

The choir stopped singing and, as the cat reached Ben, she looked up at him beguilingly, and miaowed a greeting of intense certainty that echoed around the empty church. Everyone laughed and clapped and, charmed by her apparent attention to him, Ben bent down and scooped her up in his arms. Purring loudly, she nestled into his shoulder, her whiskers tickling his ear. Father John-Henry came over to Ben and Chloe and stroked the cat gently under the chin.

'Your mother thought you'd be able to help me out of this pickle. But, Ben,' Father John-Henry gave Ben a quizzical look, 'I haven't heard you say that you want this responsibility?'

73

The cat grew restless at this point and Ben let her go back to the floor, where she started a meticulous groom of her glorious tail. Ben's mind was whirring in response to the priest's question. If he was going to say no, now was the moment. He really *did* have a choice! But he was haunted by the knowledge that the cat was to go to a cattery if no home could be found. As he watched her she turned her eyes on him again and his heart missed a beat.

'No – I do want her to come to us. I mean, um, yes, I would, I do want the responsibility. Definitely. Yes.' And, looking the priest straight in the eyes, he nodded his head.

'Last chance, Ben. You're really sure?'

'Yes, honestly I am. I really am.' Ben smiled shyly and Father John-Henry smiled back, clearly relieved.

'OK, so have you thought of a name for her yet? I always called her "Cat", so I guess I knew someone else would come along and find a proper name for her.' Father John was bending down to help Ben open up the cat carrier as he said this.

'Do you think I could call her Magnificat?' Ben said. 'It was so weird that the choir was singing that word over and over again as we came in – kind of like Magnificent Cat?'

Chloe jumped in excitedly before anyone else got a chance to speak. 'That's such an ace name – she *is* a magnificent cat!'

Ben grinned at Chloe as he gently lifted the cat down from his shoulder into the carrier. As soon as Cat realised what had happened she gave a loud miaow of protest as the lid closed down on her.

'Father John–Henry, do say it would be a good name. It would be, wouldn't it?' Chloe was tugging on his sleeve as she said this. The choir had started up again and the words *'Magnificat anima mea Dominum,'* filled the air.

'I think Magnificat would be an excellent name for your cat, Ben,' Father John-Henry said, straightening up. 'But it doesn't mean magnificent cat. The Magnificat is the Song of Mary and it is what she sang when she and her cousin Elizabeth met and knew they were both going to have babies. It was her way of praising God and of saying "Yes" to all that he was asking of her.'

It seemed that Magnificat really was the perfect name for her. And, Ben supposed, it looked like he was willing to say yes to this little cat. Magnificat, yes!

8

THE PRESENT

Magnificat felt at ease in Ben's house as soon as she was released from her carrier. She trusted this new boy in her life and his scent was everywhere in the house, so what was his, was now hers, obviously.

On her first night, as Ben started to look as if he was going to go to bed, the little cat watched him carefully. At the priest's house there had been an iron gate preventing her from going upstairs but here, it seemed, no room was barred. She followed Ben up the stairs and padded after him as he went into the bathroom and brushed his teeth. He glanced at her, waving his brush at her playfully, but he didn't say anything. He walked out, leaving the door open. She followed him across the landing and crept after him around his bedroom door, curious to see what would happen next. Ben got into bed and patted the duvet next to him. Magnificat felt uncertain and remained sitting on the floor with her tail wrapped round her paws. Ben shrugged.

'Suit yourself,' he said and putting the light out, he pulled the duvet up around his shoulders and turned over on his side to sleep. Magnificat licked her nose excitedly and decided to go for it. She sprung lightly on to the bed, turned round once, and nestled herself cosily into the bend behind his knees on top of the duvet. It was a wonderful way to spend the night. It was how she would always spend the night.

But all was not quite perfect. In the morning, Magnificat came downstairs and found the door was shut. She miaowed to be let out again and again. It was really important, she *needed* to get out. She was used to coming and going outside whenever she wanted, but in this house, for reasons she couldn't fathom, they kept the doors shut and wouldn't allow her out at all. Ben and his mum both told her that she must learn patience, soon it would be all right. They tweaked her tail and laughed. Their kindly words floated above her head like an impenetrable cloud.

At last, after some sustained mewling, Magnificat was shown a cat litter tray filled with tiny, white, plastic granules, but it was hardly the same as the soft earth. Using a tray inside was strangely embarrassing. Having lived as a free creature to find herself shut inside went quite against her nature. After that first morning she learned to wait until Ben and his mother were absent before using her litter tray – unseen by anyone – and dig, dig, dig to try to cover it up. It was strange being shut in the house on her own all day, but she spent most of her time sleeping and Ben and his mum would reappear in the late afternoon, when she would be fed and fussed over.

On Magnificat's third day at Ben's house a man came and fiddled with tools around the bottom of the door that opened into the outside world. Magnificat watched him carefully, but he made loud, jarring noises with drilling machinery that frightened her into running away to creep deep under Ben's duvet and keep safe.

After the noisy man left, she heard Ben calling for her, but she stayed where she was. Eventually Ben came into his bedroom and, although she was hidden in his bed, as he called her she gave the game away by purring loudly. Laughing, Ben uncovered her and carried her downstairs where, talking to her gently all the time, he showed her what the man had made – a small door just for her. It was a little while before she properly understood what it was, but once she did, Magnificat spent the rest of the day clicking open the swinging flap, going out and coming back in, until both Ben and his mother begged her to stop. Soon after that the litter tray was taken away and the little cat was once again the free creature she had always been.

Magnificat, now able to come inside and out at will, felt happier as she started to settle into her new home, although she remained apprehensive about how long it would last. From day one, she adored being with Ben. She could still feel a reserve in him but, as a creature whose thoughts were focussed mainly on the here and now, the little cat delighted in each close encounter as it happened, and when she did consider it, she knew that her boy would respond to her trust in him . . . soon.

If a day passed without her having achieved the cuddles she yearned for, she would never see a night through without spending some of it curled up close to the sleeping Ben. His body radiated a heat that she craved and she found his proximity comforting – usually she above the duvet and he below – on odd occasions the other way about.

Magnificat had been living with Ben less than a week when one night, as she slept curled tightly in the crook of his leg, he unintentionally kicked out in his sleep, waking her from her own deep slumbers. She let out a long protesting '*mneeeeeeeeeow*', but as his legs thrashed around, she rode out her position like an experienced bronco rider.

After a while her loud protest got through to him, causing him to open an eye. In the gloom, when he saw her eyes glowing at him, he grinned as he offered her a mock-purr in return. He did it completely wrong, but as he stretched out to stroke her, she lifted her head and her throat thrummed with a deep full-blooded feline purr, showing him exactly how it should be done.

Although Magnificat spent every night in Ben's room she wasn't always asleep. Some nights she would go outside for a brief hunting expedition, or downstairs to have a good scratch at the sofa. When she got back to Ben's room she would look for his school bag. If it was open she loved to nose around in it. It contained pens to play with and it was rich with interesting smells from another world. Mostly, though, the little cat would lie on the bed or simply sit very still and watch Ben, absorbing Ben and all his pent-up emotions until the pain that was deep within him became her own.

As well as hurt and confused, Ben also felt isolated and Magnificat recognised what he felt as only a true kindred soul can. She too was lonesome. She watched him for long stretches of the night and sometimes she was overwhelmed and would walk along his pillow and mew plaintively near his ear, only to fall quiet again as she saw the boy thrash around, hearing her call in his sleep, but not in tune with her enough to surface from his dreams. Time was what she needed – time.

Magnificat found Ben's mother considerate and kind and more often than not it was she who remembered when it was that the little cat was due her feed, which Magnificat unfailingly acknowledged with a low, clipped '*mneeow*' as it was placed before her. But Ben's mother was wary of close contact and if Magnificat ever jumped on her knee, she would quickly stand up, flicking hairs from her clothes as she did so, and forcing the little cat to jump to the ground. Once Magnificat understood the problem, she stopped doing it.

A thing she did that made Ben's mum shout (which the little cat just couldn't stop) was to brazenly hook her front claws into the soft fabric of the sofa in the front room. It was exactly the right texture to remove those irritating outer husks that covered her long, curled claws. Magnificat would sashay up to the side of the sofa and look to left and right, then stand up on her hind legs and inject the side of the sofa, front claws extended. If no one stopped her, she would get enormous pleasure from pressing them in claw by claw. It made a great sound, a cross between ripping and popping. If she was spotted she knew that Ben's mum would carry on about it and, although she often pretended she had no idea what the fuss was about, she knew *really*. When she could remember, she saved clawing the furniture for the hours of darkness or when the house was empty – it felt too good to stop completely. And, sometimes, even when they were there, she still *had* to do it.

Very soon after she had moved into Ben's house Magnificat began to develop a series of morning rituals, one of which was to greet Ben's mother the moment she heard that the kettle was switched on. She would jump on to the kitchen units and, if she was quick, there would be a little square bag hanging inside the empty mug with a dear little string on the outside, just waiting to be hooked out. The trick was to get there before the boiling hot water was poured over it, otherwise you couldn't play with it any more. When Ben's mother caught the cat doing this she laughed. She had a nice laugh.

Magnificat, once confident in her surroundings, thoroughly investigated her new territory. The little garden at the back of the house didn't provide much in the way of successful hunting as there was little or no cover in which she could stalk. But when she travelled further afield she discovered that several of the gardens in the estate had (potential) treasures hidden behind their fences. Most promising of all was a nearby pond – who knew what that might harbour once the weather grew warmer? On one of her forays she visited the church and its walled garden, but she found neither Father John-Henry nor any trace of cat food, so she left as quietly as she had arrived.

Once Magnificat had been given her freedom to the outside world she got used to the idea that Ben would disappear quite early in the morning, but she was curious to know where he went. She noticed that before he left he always took with him the bag that contained the pens and the exciting smells of some other place. One day, unable to contain her curiosity a moment longer, Magnificat followed him down the street at a discreet distance, but his route led him towards the noisy streets of the town, so she stopped and went back to the house. But she always sensed the moment when he would appear again, and so she took to sitting on a fencepost near their house, where she had a view down the street and could see the progress of his return – and return he always did.

Free to come and go as she pleased, Magnificat felt very protective of this new security; it felt precious to her. While she had been alone and frightened in the Town she had thought, longingly, of the home in which she had once lived, but it had been the place, more than the people, that had called to her. Now she felt she had found a person whom she might love. She would not easily now be parted from her boy and his mother. Within a single week this house had become not only her new home – but her complete world.

Ben, on the other hand, found himself thoroughly confused by the presence of his unwanted and unexpected early Christmas present. Away from the church and the magic of the choir singing their hymn, he felt irritated once more, not so much by the cat herself, but more by the fact that she was his present. Somehow, he felt, he had been stitched up. He had been used. Put upon. Duped.

But even as these dark thoughts crowded in, one on top of the other, he had to allow that there was *something* about her. There was an intensity to her presence. Her golden, almond-shaped eyes haunted him. They seemed to bore into him. When she was near he could feel an aura; some vague power that seemed almost to cast a spell over him.

Such conflicting emotions left him unsure whether the little cat was good news or not. This turmoil within Ben meant that whenever Magnificat approached him he would sometimes give her the caresses she sought and at other times he actively shunned her. She never seemed to mind and he wondered if she even noticed. One day, just before the holidays, he thought he saw her sitting on a fencepost in the road waiting for him . . . but he decided he probably imagined it.

Two days before Christmas the weather turned cold once more with heavy snow forecast. Just before school broke up, some of his classmates had been arguing whether this one would be the long-awaited white Christmas. Ben didn't know whether he minded one way or the other. So what if it was white? Christmas always seemed to be a lot of fuss about nothing.

Ben dreaded the state his mother got into trying to organise the big Christmas dinner – even though there were only two of them! If last year was anything to go by, it would surely turn itself into a major drama with Mum ending up in floods of tears and saying everything was hopeless and wanting to go to bed. Dad always tried to come over and that caused its own tensions because he was so unreliable. Last year he simply didn't turn up at all and Mum had told him she thought it was because Tracy, Dad's girlfriend, had put her foot down.

So as the day approached, Ben braced himself for the big build-up and the great let-down. Yet again, this year his dad was staying true to form. He just didn't seem able to make up his mind about what on Earth he was doing. Tomorrow was Christmas Eve, so it was then or never.

As Ben pulled back his curtains, he saw the snow tumbling down out of a grey sky in great, soft, silent flakes. They were large and steady and looked as if they meant business. He entered the front room with Magnificat draped around the back of his neck – her choice not his – just as the phone went. His mother picked it up and Ben could hear his dad's voice on the other end. He was talking fast and laughing, but Ben's mum wasn't. She sighed and put the phone down, looking sadly across at Ben. His dad would come over straightaway and head back before dark. No time to stay for the planned Christmas Eve dinner, they would just have a quick midday snack.

'Ben – it's for the best. Your dad is just frightened that the road is going to get closed with the drifting snow before he gets back!'

Ben shrugged. It wasn't a big deal. Mum walked across the room and ruffled his hair, which annoyed him, but he realised she was trying to be kind. There was no doubt that his dad was totally useless.

An hour later Dad arrived in his van and the three of them sat down to a hasty meal of beans on toast. Dad seemed to be in a jolly mood and after they had eaten he grabbed Ben by the arm. Ben saw him wink at Mum as he called him over to the van. The snow was still falling steadily and settling and their feet made scrunchy noises as they walked.

'I've got something for you.' Dad glanced over at Mum and pulled an apologetic face. 'Well, truth is that it's from us both.' He opened the sliding door of the van.

'Oh, Charlie, you could have let me wrap it up first, for heaven's sake!' Mum said. Dad pushed out his bottom lip in mock remorse and slapped the back of his hand to his brow, then grinned. As Ben peered into the gloom of the van he could hardly believe his eyes. There, lying in solitary splendour in a slightly battered box, was a brand new mobile phone. It didn't matter that it wasn't wrapped up. After believing that the cat was the only present he was getting, he really hadn't believed that anything else was going to come his way. As he turned, his face wreathed in smiles, his dad held up his hands.

'Before you ask, it has a memory card and there are also a few games on it, but you'll have to find someone else to play with you.'

'Oh, Dad, thank you, thank you!' Ben jumped up and down with pleasure and flung his arms around his beaming Dad.

'You'd better thank your mum too, it's from us both,' Dad murmured quietly. Ben walked up to his mum and squeezed her arm.

'Mum, thank you. That is a really cool present. Thank you!'

His mum drew breath as if she was going to say something and, relaxing a little, gave him a weak grin. Ben rushed round and took pictures of his mum and his dad until they both begged him to leave off.

As their voices and laughter drifted into the house, Magnificat, who had been asleep on Ben's bed all morning, emerged through the cat flap and sniffed at the snow. Ben made the formal introductions and his Dad said he was pleased to meet her having heard all about her from Mum.

'Well!' Dad said. 'Aren't you a gorgeous girl?' He leaned down to tweak her tail. She miaowed politely, but quickly whisked her tail out of harm's way. Ben laughed.

'You don't have to go over the top, Dad. I mean she's all right. For a cat . . . I guess.'

Ben's dad bent down to scoop up a handful of the snow and threw it gently for the little cat. She bounded after it with glee and snuffled at it wetly, trying to eat it. Ben and his dad laughed together as Ben scooped up some snow. Mum smiled as she watched father and son and cat at play. As she went inside she heard their renewed bellows of laughter and saw the amazing image of Magnificat squatting erect on her back legs determinedly fielding a ball with her front paws that would otherwise have hit her broadsides on. Ben, who had been clicking away with his new toy was thrilled to discover when he checked that he had captured Magnificat for all time performing a catch of outstanding brilliance.

Dad left shortly after and, later, Ben was amused to receive his first ever text message:

Got back ok – road closing up behind me – enjoy your phone – Happy Christmas tomorrow – love Dad.

When Christmas Day actually arrived the meal of turkey and trimmings originally intended to be shared with Dad was eaten by Ben and Mum in companionable silence, watching the white light reflected through the windows of their little house.

It felt like a good, calm, gentle sort of day and Mum didn't get stressed out, not even once.

As Ben handed over his Christmas present of mixed soaps to his mum and she said thank you in a really nice way, he wished he had put a bit more thought into it.

Mum had bought a packet of small plastic balls with holes and little bells inside for Magnificat, which she gave to Ben to give the cat, which made Ben feel a bit guilty, as it had never occurred to him to get the cat anything. It was the first time that Ben had ever seen a cat play football. He was surprised at her dribbling skills and it made him laugh, although she was a terrible cheat and would pick the ball up in her claws. Certainly Magnificat enjoyed the gift. So all in all it was a good Christmas for all three.

On Boxing Day Ben briefly visited Josh to show off his mobile and was thrilled at how impressed Josh was with the touch-screen, much better than his, he said. Later that night, as Ben lay in bed, he smiled broadly into the darkness. His hand was resting lightly on Magnificat and he could feel the rise and fall of her rib cage as she breathed. Her tongue rasped the back of his hand and the hairs stood up on his neck at the sensation of her caress. He laughed out loud, but his enormous grin had been at the memory of what happened a couple of hours ago. Back from Josh's, Ben had bounced into the house, where he found his mother in the kitchen. He'd crept up behind her and put his arms around her and given her a bear hug. She had her hands in the sink and she had spoken without turning round.

'And what was that for, might I ask, young man?'

'It was to say a whopping great big thank you. Thank you

for a great Christmas and thank you because you gave me the cat and then you and Dad gave me the mobile. And I know I didn't deserve it or anything. And I didn't expect it. And, and, well . . . it's great. Thank you Mum.'

Standing on his tiptoes, Ben leaned forward across the draining board so he could see her face.

'Mum,' he said shyly, 'I do love you.'

And that was when she had turned towards him and given him a smile that lit up the whole wide world.

PART II

9

THE ENTERTAINER

The old year saw itself out under a cold mantle of snow, but with the new there came a total change in the weather. Gone were the hard frosts and treacherous silent snowfalls of December and now, instead, fierce shafts of stinging rain blustered in on the Atlantic gales. It was the sort of weather that turned umbrellas inside out and made people scurry for cover the way ants do when a log is rolled away.

Boy and cat alike were more than happy to spend the remainder of Ben's Christmas holidays inside the little house in the warmth and the dry, well away from those disturbing winds. Magnificat became increasingly skilful at working out when the moment was right to cosy up to Ben. She had an almost inexhaustible desire to play games and she discovered that if she hooked her paw round Ben's finger at the right moment it would make him laugh and he might be distracted enough from whatever he was doing to stop and play with her. If not, then there was always later.

Magnificat very quickly learned how to read Ben's moods. When she could sense his heart was at rest she would quietly worm her way on to his knee and, once there, she would creep up on to his arms which, when he was really at peace, he would helpfully fold into a platform for her. From that vantage point she could stand up on her back legs, rest her front paws on his shoulder and nuzzle into the warm spot in his neck, behind his ear, and breathe him in. Sometimes she would lick his hair in a gentle pulling motion, because her tongue was covered in tiny little hooks especially made for grooming – like a built-in hairbrush. So skilled did she become at nurturing her boy that soon she could even influence his moods a little.

Over and above his smell, which had beguiled her since the first time she had met him, there was something in him which stirred her; something that she had never before encountered. As well as an instinctive gentleness that allowed her to trust him completely, Ben had a vulnerability which, without her understanding it, had a compelling effect upon her. When he held her, his hands were so, so soft. He stroked her in such a way – tender and barely touching her – that made her feel greatly cherished. This was a new emotion for Magnificat and it thrilled her. There was a special place where she loved to be caressed, beneath the base of her ear and under her jaw and when Ben found it, he stroked her until she purred what seemed like an endless song of happiness in return. If Ben had been especially caring, she would gently drool with pleasure as her eyes stared dreamily into the distance.

Then there were the headbutts. Magnificat really needed to headbutt Ben to show her trust of him. Sometimes she did it gently and sometimes she did it with force. One time it would be his leg, another his head, and most often of all the back of his hand. She felt a strong need to make contact with him – almost a compulsion – to put her own scent on him, so making him hers.

And, slowly, Magnificat started to receive small rewards back from her boy Ben. One was his laugh. It was a special laugh, sort of quiet and private. A laugh as gentle as a puff of wind.

Just before school went back, Josh came over and Chloe tagged along to see how Magnificat was settling down, and – being tuned into cats – she brought with her a packet of catnip. On entering the house, Chloe announced she had magic to execute. As she walked forward, she rolled up both her sleeves as if she was going to perform some conjuring trick, and slowly peppered the chopped-up leaves over the sofa cushions.

'Watch this. It won't last for more than a few seconds, a minute at most, but the effect is awesome!'

Indeed. Magnificat who had been lying on her favourite chair, not paying much attention to anyone, suddenly miaowed loudly, almost rudely. Her delicate nose wrinkled up as she smelled the catnip. With astonishing speed she leaped across the room on to the sofa where she promptly devoured a mouthful of it. Before any of them knew what was happening she had turned about and rolled on top of the herb, first one way, then the other, finally ending up in a silly position on her back, with her paws extended, gazing up at the ceiling. Her eyes were glistening and she had a dreamy expression in them. Ben was astonished.

'That's completely amazing. What's in it?' Ben gasped. He took the packet from Chloe and taking out a pinch of the herb he sniffed and licked it. Boring! Tea leaves were more interesting! He looked back at the little cat. Magnificat was definitely, unquestionably, magnificently happy. And then she rolled over, stood up, and jumped down, exactly as if nothing at all had happened. It was all over.

'Well, Ben! I reckon that's the real difference between us and cats. Nice one, Chlo!' Josh said. 'Bet it wouldn't work on Clueless though!'

'We can try when we get home, but it would be called dognip if it did, wouldn't it?' Chloe said, as she tossed her ponytail triumphantly, grinning. 'I'd better clean up the mess, before your Mum sees it. Is she working round at the new priest's today?'

'Yes,' Ben said.

'Have you met him?' Chloe said, 'Father John-Henry he *isn't*!' They chatted a bit about Father John-Henry whose operation had gone well and who was now recovering from it all in a monastery somewhere by the sea.

What Ben really wanted to do was show off the talents that he knew Magnificat possessed as a ball player so, rather brutally grabbing her by her long tail from under the table, he hauled her into full view. Magnificat mewled out in protest and smacked Ben's hand away with her paw, scrabbling back under the table. Chloe was appalled and ticked Ben off, saying it didn't matter how well he got on with the cat, pulling her around by her tail was completely out of order. Leaning forward she looked at Ben fiercely as she put her hands on her hips. Ben had to hold in a grin. Chloe could be quite scary.

'It would jolly well serve you right if that little pusscat just upped sticks and went walkies.' Ben rolled his eyes, but the incident made him even more determined to show off his cat's skills. To begin with Magnificat refused to come out from under the table – she really hadn't liked being manhandled in that way – but as Ben teased the ball back and forth she relented and began to pat at it, ever more keenly.

She was astonishingly adept at batting it first with her left paw and then her right all around the room. Her spectators were transfixed as they watched her skilful dribbling. But it was when Ben picked the ball up and threw it a good distance that she most impressed her audience. She raced after it, but as soon as she caught up with it, she unabashedly hooked her claws through the holes and 'held' the ball aloft for all to see before, still clasping the ball in her claws, she shuffled back on three legs to Ben, only to release her claws and drop it neatly at his feet for a further throw.

'That isn't soccer, Magnificat! That's some cheating sort-of rugby for heaven's sake,' Josh protested.

'Hey! Shut up, you – I think it's brilliant!' Chloe countered, admiringly. Ben put his head down, but he was grinning with pleasure. He wasn't convinced that a cat in any way shaped up compared with a dog, but nevertheless he felt absurdly pleased with his little cat for performing her party trick so well.

10

THE FROGS

As the month of February began, gentle warm westerlies prevailed. Bands of steady rain folded softly across the land in misty veils. With the milder temperature and the longer days, much of the wildlife that had been hibernating started to surface and, with so many more creatures active, the hunting possibilities for a young predator were much enhanced. Life outside the house was becoming increasingly interesting.

So interesting, indeed, that Magnificat developed a new passion: frogs. Big frogs, little frogs, brown frogs, green frogs, any sort of frog within a quarter of a mile was under threat from her. And she had no mercy. She had learned her way around the network of gardens within the estate and her particular favourite was the one on the corner of her road – the one that contained the big pond.

The warmer weather had kick-started the female frogs into creeping out of their boggy hidey-holes and seeking out their various breeding ponds. Several of them knew well that the best spot was the garden on the corner. It suited them because the pond contained lush plant cover and half of it had a shelf providing shallow water, which both tadpoles and young frogs would enjoy.

Magnificat's strange taste for the common frog had started innocently enough. She had encountered them as they first came out of hibernation. Their strange mode of locomotion – great high springy jumps – fascinated her and by nosing them along in front of her she found that she could accurately guess the length and direction of their leap. It was great sport.

To begin with she had been content merely to chase them. But one day the frog she was chasing started to emit the strange screaming noise that frogs make when in danger to try to distract the hunter. Instead of being put off, Magnificat lunged forward and grabbed the frog, more to quieten than to kill him, but frogs are exceptionally soft bodied, as she discovered when she pierced him and, in so doing, killed him. She chewed off one of the legs and found that it tasted good; so good that she became quite addicted to frogs' legs. Now, forsaking all other prey, she would sit in the long grass of the garden lawns, making use of all her senses: smell, hearing and sight, but especially her deeply embedded whiskers, whose many nerve endings would detect the change in air. By experience now, she would be able to tell when frogs were near to her without even turning her head.

One day Magnificat was chasing an especially bright green frog, who, feeling somewhat overwhelmed by her, flipped over on his back shamming death, barely breathing. Such froggy play-acting usually deterred a normal predator, but not the tenacious Magnificat. Knowing he was alive, she went in for the kill anyway.

Now, with the breeding season in full swing, Magnificat would spend long stretches of time sitting close enough to the pond to see all that was going on. The noise level as each frog tried to out-croak the other would build up into a crescendo, and the ground nearby vibrated with the deep purring sounds coming from the water. As the calls climaxed, the pond would become quite riotous, with the surface of the water rocking violently from side to side while the male frogs chased the females around. One of the females had two male frogs clamped to her back waiting for her to lay her spawn and Magnificat looked on with awe. She watched the trio moving around the pond with keen attention, but to her disappointment they never came ashore – and she firmly resisted the temptation to enter the water. Even a prize of three frogs in one pounce wasn't worth getting wet over.

Whilst pond-watching, the cat would usually conceal herself from her prey under a clump of thick bushes. One day, when she accidentally became visible bending down to drink from the pond, she heard an angry voice and at the same moment she felt the wet sting of pressured water as it hit her in her ribs. She turned and saw a man bearing down on her aiming a hosepipe directly at her! She ran from the scene like a scared rabbit and from that time on she made sure it wasn't just the frogs who were innocent of her whereabouts.

In spite of her newfound lust for frogs, Magnificat remained as enchanted as ever by her boy Ben and spent most of each night curled close to his sleeping form. As part of her deep respect for him she had twice taken a living frog back to him as a present. His reaction had been strange as on both occasions he had taken them away from her and let them go free where she couldn't find them. He obviously hadn't understood. Now, if she wanted to please him, she took him dead ones as presents, which he seemed to prefer. It was hard to be sure.

As before, Ben spent evenings and weekends at Josh's house, where the boys would spend hours playing on the computer. Occasionally they allowed Chloe to join them, but more often than not she was out with her own friends. Whenever Ben met her she always asked him how Magnificat was doing, which made him feel uncomfortable although he wasn't sure why. Sometimes their classmates Mohammed and Dan joined them and Josh's mother would mildly complain that the decibel levels coming from Josh's room were like those of the playground. Whenever it became too much for her, the boys would meet at Ben's, when Magnificat was always invited to play football with them. She seemed to enjoy their company while they focussed on her, but the noise they made once they played their own games would ultimately drive her away.

Still, most of all, Ben loved the days when he and Josh went off together with Clueless. Clueless was brilliant. You could make him do things – anything. He would swim through water again and again even when it was really cold. The only trouble was that whenever he made land again he always shook himself all over you. He would do everything you told him to, even if it wasn't actually a good idea. He was brilliant at bringing back big sticks, jumping for joy and barking and generally being fun. The most amazing thing about Clueless was that he behaved as if Josh, and by extension Ben, were god-like beings. It felt wonderful to be completely adored.

Every so often when Ben returned home, tired and muddy from wild cavorting down at the river bank, his face aching from too much laughter, he would stroke his patient little cat and look at her, through half-closed eyes, and wish really hard that she was something other than a cat – like maybe a dog. There was nothing of her for a start. She was all long fur, big tail and whiskers finished off by tiny dainty feet – if a big puff of wind blew, it would be easy to believe that she might be carried away on it with no trouble at all.

When Ben studied her like that she would look back at him steadily, holding his gaze and give him the big, silent miaow. That silent miaow was her secret weapon. Ben, without realising it, always melted when she did that. It was as if she was saying something secretly to him and him alone. It touched his heart – just a little bit – then he would give her his special soft laugh in return and, when he did, she jumped towards him and licked his hair, her deep purrs echoing around his ears.

As the weeks that Magnificat spent in Ben's house grew

into months, Ben thought about the way she was and how she showed her feelings. It was very different from the love a dog gives. It was gentler and somehow more private.

Some of her faults were quite doglike, though. For instance those horrible frogs she kept bringing back. They were so disgusting – and it was a *shame*. Frogs, living frogs that is, were nice. It had been all right at the beginning, when they weren't injured and he could let them go free again, but then she started bringing them back dead, and often with bits missing, such as half a leg or no head. The worst moment of all was when she'd left a mutilated dead frog by his bed, so when he got out of bed in the morning he trod on it with his bare feet. Awful! It was cold and squashy and slippery and disgusting and he'd had to go and wash and wash and wash his feet in the bath to make absolutely sure it had all gone.

Ben remembered how Clueless, too, treated frogs. Josh had once kicked a dead frog – probably killed by a car – into the gutter out of the way. Some time later, when it had gone smelly, Clueless had discovered it and rolled in it so he really stank, then, that not being enough, he'd eaten it. Worse, after he'd eaten it, he was sick before eating that too! Ben grinned as he recalled this. On second thoughts, cats weren't really as disgusting as dogs.

The other thing that Clueless did, which embarrassed Ben quite a lot, was shove his nose into people's crotches, *really* obviously. It didn't matter whether they were grown-ups or children, male or female, it appeared to be all the same to Clueless. Whereas with Magnificat she only wanted to scent-mark you, and Ben had to admit, it was considerably less violent. In fact she often did it without you realising she was doing it, by encouraging you to stroke her and then gently rubbing her face and her ears over the bits of you that she deemed should smell of her.

As he thought about that he suddenly realised that was *why* she walked where she walked. He had been aware over the weeks of how she would seem to collide with him. He knew full well that his little cat had a superb sense of distance and balance, so why did she do it? Ben laughed as he realised that she simply wanted to keep reinforcing her scent on him and all the prominent bits of furniture around the place.

Ben was lying in bed as he had this profound realisation and he turned to stare at Magnificat. She gazed back at him with a great aura of calm, then closed her eyes. Ben, too, closed his eyes, then opened them again quickly to see her watching him, wide-eyed. It gave him the strangest feeling. As if she could read his thoughts. As if she knew and understood things about him that he didn't himself. It made him shiver.

As Ben snuggled down below the duvet, he felt her wriggling beside him and very gently he felt the tickle of her long, silky fur touch the bare skin of his tummy where his pyjama top had pulled up. She was actually under the duvet in bed with him. He felt her move around, getting comfortable until she found a curvy bit of him where she could snuggle and she curled up and went totally still. This felt so soft and warm and trusting that Ben glowed with love. As he drifted towards a companionable sleep, he hoped darkly that it wasn't all too good to be true.

11

THE FIGHT

Spring was now in full spate. The world was teeming with action and what had begun with the raucous amphibians had now spread to bird, reptile, insect and mammal alike. In every quarter animal life was vital and calling. The air vibrated with the sounds and displays of creatures looking for a mate and it was no longer frogs that were at the forefront of Magnificat's mind. She was disturbed and restless and found herself, without thinking, wandering greater distances every day. Unsure of what she was seeking, the little cat felt driven to explore. She found herself torn between two urges. Although she was strongly drawn to her boy Ben, she felt an overwhelming need to seek her own kind.

One night, having spent the first half of it on Ben's bed, Magnificat was seized more powerfully than ever before by the desire to roam. The little cat miaowed quietly as she made up her mind and, without waking the sleeping boy, she set off.

First Magnificat made her way around the edge of the town to avoid the main roads and wandered down to the wide, twisting river. She sat on the riverside watching the water tumbling over the thousands of pebbles that made up its bed.

Magnificat loved the sound the myriad drops of water made as they chattered their way across and between the stones. She sat – body erect and perfectly still – while her ears flicked rapidly to pick up the sounds above the gurgles of running water. Her nose twitched as she breathed in the smells around her and her tail trembled in suspense. Immediately Magnificat recognised the moment she was no longer alone and turned her head, nerve endings alive. There she saw the light, glowing shape of a cat, enormous and long-haired and pure white.

White miaowed a greeting to Magnificat and she quietly returned it. Magnificat could sense the heat of his body through her whiskers. As her blood thudded in her ears she looked at him and realised that this was what she had been waiting for; she had, unknowingly, been seeking a mate. She mewled a second greeting, but White didn't respond. He was sitting some distance from her and remained there with his tail wrapped primly around his front feet. Magnificat changed her tone into a loud basso yowl. White blinked, but he didn't move a muscle.

Magnificat was surprised, as she knew he must have sought her out specifically. Why did he ignore her clear invitation to come closer? She moved towards him slowly and, standing opposite, she rolled on the ground in front of him. White stood up and gently approached the female cat to lick her nose and, slowly, she licked him back. He nuzzled into her neck and she was about to respond when a low guttural growling started close by. Magnificat leaped back. White didn't react at first, then he suddenly swung round.

An even larger tom than White emerged darkly from the shadows. He was pure black, both ears ragged from fighting, and he bore a large scar over one eye. Black's tail thrashed the ground and his fur stood on end over every inch of his body making him seem enormous. His frayed ears rotated in an agitated manner, but then tipped forward and Magnificat saw his great yellow eyes gleaming in the dark. He changed his guttural growling into a strange yowl straight into White's face. White flared back at Black, flattening his ears threateningly.

Magnificat remained silent. She had never felt so totally alive in all her life. The sound that the two toms were making made every nerve in her body stand on end. It was the most wonderful serenade in the world, filled with threat, promise, aggression, love and hate. Although the toms were facing each other initially, White started to show his flank to Black, and Black, older and more experienced, took the advantage this weakness allowed him. He put his head down towards Magnificat and moved his big shoulders towards her. She watched him and slightly lowered her head, mewling at him prettily. Her call determined his next action.

Black swung round and slashed out violently at White, who hissed back in shock and backed off to fade away into the shadows. Victorious, Black turned to Magnificat and licked her and she returned his greeting. Soon the pair mated. They continued to caper and chase and mate throughout the night, until shortly before dawn, when Black licked Magnificat's nose farewell and started his sedate journey home, returning downstream and crossing the river at Devil's Bridge.

Magnificat too was ready for home and, having groomed herself, she looked around to see if there was any sign of White. On seeing nothing, she returned to her estate and to Ben, where she crept up on to his bed and tucked herself close to the warm round mound that was her sleeping boy. By the time Ben awoke the little cat was fast asleep.

Later that morning Magnificat woke up hungry. Ben was nowhere to be seen so she took herself downstairs and ate the dried biscuits that had been left out for her. Pausing, she thought she could hear a cat calling and, after navigating her way through the cat flap, to her surprise and delight, she saw that White was waiting for her, and in his mouth he held a large, dead, rat. He offered his love gift to her and she took it gratefully – so much better than biscuits! When she had nearly finished eating, he came across and ate a little himself.

After they had each groomed themselves they then, gently, mated. And that was when she discovered that White was stone deaf. He was clever at compensating for his lack of hearing, which is why she had not realised when first she met him, but it explained why the large black tom had found it easy to take advantage, since the younger white tom could only sense the growling warnings when he was looking straight on. Magnificat, however, was much taken with her white friend, whose gentle ways were more to her liking than the forthright Black. It pleased her too, that he had troubled to pursue her scent all the way back from the river.

For the next day and the next night, White remained lurking around the bushes near Magnificat's house and the two cats spent much time together.

Magnificat did not, however, entirely forget about Black. On the third night of White's courtship Magnificat heard the most terrible sound of tom cats in a no-holds-barred cat fight. She recognised the two voices raised in anger. The spat seemed to last a long time and the small female cowered inside as she heard the howls and the spittings until, finally, all went quiet. Magnificat crept outside. As she walked around the wall of the small garden, she came face to face with Black. He was licking a newly acquired wound, but the moment he saw Magnificat he stopped his grooming and greeted her warmly. That night Magnificat belonged to Black once more.

The following day a change came over the little female. Having had enough attention from her two courtiers, she decided to spend her time indoors, close to Ben. Ben responded affectionately to the renewed interest that Magnificat showed him and that night they slept the whole night with the boy's hand on the little cat's side, undisturbed.

As Ben slept with a tiny smile on his lips, Magnificat twitched violently and mewled out in her sleep. She was dreaming of a long spiralling column of black cats snaking away in one direction and another spiral of white cats in the other. She could hear them calling to her and they all wanted her to play . . . only she didn't know which column to follow.

12

THE WATCHER

Ben realised one day that Magnificat had excellent manners. It hit him out of the blue as he and Josh were throwing sticks for the inexhaustible Clueless. It was the dog who made him see it. Clueless would simply bark louder and louder if he wanted things, but he never barked a thank you. If you opened a door to let Magnificat in she would pass by and make a quite distinct '*mneeeow*' of thanks. And it was always the same tone and the same sound for that particular action. It was a special mew of thanks. She never failed.

'No one's told her she's got to do it. She just does because she wants to. Don't you think that's cute?' Ben said. Josh laughed and told Ben he wasn't convinced.

'On the other hand,' Ben admitted, 'if it rains she blames

me, which is crazy as she must know I don't control the weather. But she looks out of the window when it's chucking it down and makes this horrible whiney sort of *mneeeow*, right at me. She can keep it up for ages.'

'Well, what about playing then?' Josh protested. 'She can't *play* as well as Clueless, surely?'

'Yes and no. She can't pick up big sticks, but there's something about the way that she plays . . . it's . . . it's like she's deliberately entertaining me. Almost.' Ben stood up from the bank the boys had been sitting on, feeling the damp seeping through the seat of his jeans and stamped his feet to get some blood circulating round his body again.

'Honestly. You've got to see it. When she plays she *becomes* play. It's like it's a part of her entire being,' he said and grinned.

Josh gave Ben a funny look and raised both eyebrows. 'Well, I reckon that's true for Clueless as well.'

'No, it's different, trust me! Clueless just wants it for him. He can't see beyond the stick.' Ben puffed out his cheeks and waved his hands in an all-embracing kind of way. 'Magnificat enters into the game until she *is* it in some weird way. It's like she's telling you to chill out, and play more yourself, that play's the thing, that's what it's about! Everything, simply *everything's* about play!'

Josh gave his friend a light-hearted shove. 'You're really turning into a proper cat-boy, you are!' When Josh said this he ducked, as if he expected Ben to clobber him, but the strangest thing was that Ben didn't object. He just grinned, soppily.

The truth of the matter was that Ben was giving more time every day to playing with his little cat and thoughts of her constantly filled his mind. And that was the thing – he really had started to think of her as *his*. When, recently, he had made the mistake of talking about Magnificat in glowing terms at school – it *had* probably sounded a bit daft – some of them had laughed at him and started to joke about his "diddums-puddytat". Ben had been hurt. Magnificat wasn't a joke. She was special and since they didn't get it, he stopped talking about her. He didn't want them calling him weird. He didn't want them calling *her* weird either. But he was desperate to find an ally. Obviously Chloe understood, but he really didn't see that much of Chloe except during classes. He had, however, noticed that Mohammed never failed to make a fuss of Magnificat when he met her. He was gentle and quiet in the way he handled her, in a cat-sensitive way, so Ben knew it would be all right to talk to him – out of school anyway.

The next time Mohammed was round at Ben's, without the others, he told Ben that he would love a cat more than anything. Although his parents weren't that keen on pets generally, he hoped they might just relent on the matter of a cat.

'Cats are respected all over Islam,' Mohammad said, as he gently stroked Magnificat. 'It's funny that you found her in a church – cats are the only animals allowed to go inside a mosque.' He looked down at Magnificat again and let out an enormous sigh of longing. 'I do think she's special. You're ever so lucky.' Magnificat looked up at this softly spoken boy as he let her tail drift slowly between his forefinger and thumb and she murmured a soft '*purrp*'. Ben smiled, proudly.

One day, as Ben was playing with Magnificat with the stick and feather, he started to try to work out *exactly* how much of his hard-earned pocket money he'd spent on cat toys. As he thought of them all he ran out of fingers to count them on.

The list included this stick with a feather attached, balls of every kind – countless cat treats, bags of dried catnip, and toy mice. The mice came in every shape and size – white fur mice, brown fur mice and her absolute favourite – a rope mouse stuffed with catnip. The next thing on Ben's list was to buy her a laser mouse . . . And this didn't even include the really useful things that she absolutely *had* to have like the padded cat bed, which she slept in downstairs during the day. He'd even thought about getting a scratching post . . . but they were very expensive.

Magnificat, or MC as he most often called her, loved all the toys he bought her, but her most cherished was the rope mouse with purple stripes round its body ending in a purple tail, with lurid green ears, an orange nose and coal-black eyes. She would become deeply troubled whenever it went missing – usually to be found under the sofa, behind the rubbish bin, or even outside in the garden.

Ben still, occasionally, tried to play ball with his little cat, but these days you couldn't guarantee she'd bring it back, so he'd stopped playing it in front of other people. He had to admit that in some ways – as a games player – his cat had become a tiny bit unreliable.

Magnificat's life was serene and happy and getting better all the time. The house was warm and friendly. She was fed whenever she needed food, usually by Ben's mother. And the affection she craved from her boy Ben was more evident day by day. She noticed that he gave her far more attention than he ever had before and that when he got in from school he spent time with her before anything else. In return she gave him her fullest consideration.

A recent toy he had introduced was something he held in his hand, which she couldn't figure out, but it made a tiny bright light dance across the floor and up the walls and even on the ceiling and she went mad for it. She could never quite catch it, but the chase was everything. He called it a laser mouse, which showed how much he knew about real mice! And there was a green feather on a stick that reminded her of the fun she had pursuing birds . . . Ben was far too slow at pulling it away in time and that had spoiled it a bit, as there weren't many feathers left now. Her boy wouldn't last long in the wild with reactions like that.

But the best toy of all was the rope mouse which had catnip in it. Magnificat spent hours scent-marking it to make sure everyone knew and understood that it was hers and that it was always where she could find it. If it went missing she became distressed and would make Ben help her find it. It was very upsetting when it got stuck *under* things and no one understood what she was trying to tell them – most frustrating.

She did wish, however, that he would give up trying to play with the ball all the time. There was no further development to that game. There was no point to it. It was boring now. She was finished with it. Why didn't he get it? Her boy should just understand. She *did* keep telling him.

One Friday evening, Ben was lying back in a deep warm bath absent-mindedly chewing the corner of his flannel and not thinking of anything at all important when Magnificat miaowed at the door to be let in. When Ben ignored her, she shoved her paw right under the door and Ben saw her claws flex and her pad open wide. He knew that once she started agitating there would be no end to it until she was in. Groaning, Ben got out of the bath dripping all over the floor and opened the door. Magnificat miaowed her thanks and jumped up, to sit primly on the corner of the bath where she stared down at the boy attentively.

Ben sank gratefully back into the warm water, but after a while he began to feel slightly uncomfortable under such intense scrutiny.

'I can't work out what you're thinking when you stare at me like that, MC. What is it?' She blinked, and looked away, but when Ben looked back at her, she was watching him again. He got out of the bath, wrapped himself in a towel and pulled her to him. This was always a special moment between them, when he stroked her under her chin and she purred deep and long. He loved this moment of closeness more than anything. Tonight was strange, though. She had seemed so badly to want the cuddle, but instead of tucking into him she gave one small mew of farewell and jumped down. Ben stood up and got ready for bed. He stamped crossly out of the bathroom, towards his room.

'Suit yourself, MC,' he said over his shoulder, adding, 'but you'll miss me when I'm gone.' As he heard his own words he screwed up his face in self-mockery. He couldn't believe he'd just said that. It was something Mum said a lot. He was turning into his mum!

Suddenly Ben heard a loud galumphing coming from inside the empty bath. He stepped back into the room and there was Magnificat turning in mad, ever-decreasing circles, chasing her tail until she was exhausted and panting. When she stopped her eyes sought out Ben's to make sure that he was taking it all in. It seemed very important to her. Ben wanted to cry with laughter, but he knew that Magnificat shouldn't realise that. She looked up at him with such a serious expression on her face, her golden eyes so large and dark that it made him shiver.

'What is it, MC? Can you see into the future? Go on. Do tell. Please!'

But of course she didn't.

Magnificat considered Ben to be in her care, and one of the things she needed to do regularly was to keep a watch over him. It was necessary to check that he was where she had last seen him, as humans had a tendency to sneak out when you weren't watching and when he went into the bathroom it was always a bit hit and miss whether the door would be left open. Magnificat always made a fuss if she knew Ben was in there and the door was shut, and she would put her whole leg under the door and wave it about until Ben opened it.

The important bit was when he got out of the bath. Then it would be good for that cuddle afterwards, which really mattered. Sometimes just thinking about the cuddle made her get excited and she would miaow loudly in anticipation. But at other times, like now, she had waited for so long and watched him so hard that by the time he got out of the bath, she just didn't want to do it any more. The moment had passed.

She immediately regretted it when Ben stamped past without seeming to notice that there had been no proper cuddle. So she ran back into the bathroom and jumped into the warm, but empty, bath and ran round wildly, faster and faster, trying to catch that tail that kept just being out of reach. Ben came back in and stood, watching her. She could feel he had laughter bubbling deep down in him. She hated, really hated, to be laughed at. She didn't like that. Not one bit. But more importantly she was trying to get across to him what she meant and then he broke it by speaking.

'What is it, MC? Can you see into the future? Go on. Do tell. Please!'

But of course she didn't.

It was Saturday and Ben had been looking forward to his first lie-in for five days. The pearl-grey light of dawn was starting to creep round the edge of the curtains as Magnificat started up the morning routine. She sat on the windowsill half behind the curtain and stared at Ben. Who knows how long she had been watching? She made a great long, loud miaow.

Ben was deeply asleep and turned as he heard it and put the pillow over his head. Magnificat jumped across to the bed and sat down next to the pillow. She started purring. Noisily, like a small motor. Ben surfaced a little bit and turned over again. Magnificat climbed on to his sleeping form and walked down the length of his body, over his rib cage and down on to his hip. She lay astride his hip. Heavily. Ben groaned and rolled around and she fell off him on to the bed. She walked up and sat next to his head again, leaning forward and patting him gently on his cheek with her politely sheathed paw. Ben slept on although his hand came up to brush her paw away. She purred a bit, then patted him again. He turned over on to his other side and Magnificat put out the very tips of her long, fierce claws through her gleaming white gloves and, just slightly, not enough to draw blood, pricked him on his upper lip. His hand moved her paw away. She did it again; this time a bit deeper. Ben shouted out, sat up and started to rub his eyes. Magnificat watched him happily and purred to him deeply until he smiled and stroked her.

This injection-by-claw never failed to work. Ben never dared to let her go beyond three stabbings. It simply hurt too much.

Magnificat had no way of understanding the difference between a school day and a weekend. All she knew was that as soon as the grey light of dawn was showing it was time for Ben to play with her. She had to work really hard to make him pay attention and would have much preferred that he woke up on his own without her having to purr and prod and prick. Although the effect of the prick-in-the-lip was always amusing.

And, if she woke him up and it turned out to be raining, which she could usually sense, she felt massively frustrated. Why didn't Ben sort it out? He could be really inattentive to important things. When he opened the door and showed it to her, she kept telling him what she thought of his horrible weather, but it never seemed to make any difference. He still made it rain.

There were so many things about Magnificat that simply melted Ben's heart. She was brave and she was feisty and she had attitude – all of which made him admire her in different ways. But, the more he studied her, the more he began to see that she was also a small, vulnerable animal with great needs, who could be easily hurt. And she possessed both pride and a sense of her own dignity, which he now knew must always be respected.

One rainy Sunday, when they had both been in a playful mood, Magnificat had started to walk towards Ben along the table edge. She had been so intent on getting him to connect with her that she wasn't watching her step at all and, misplacing her front foot she fell, quite clumsily, to the floor. Briskly she picked herself up, looked at Ben and sprung back on the table. Then, to his lasting delight, she did the same thing again, this time landing neatly, to show him that she had intended to do it all along. Fall first, then land neatly. It was what cats did. Ben had laughed openly at her when she looked across at him, and told her she hadn't fooled him for one moment. Clearly offended, she turned her back to him, sat down, stretched her back leg into a line pointing straight up to heaven and nonchalantly groomed herself. That had taught Ben to be really careful not to laugh. Magnificat did not like that. Not one bit.

One of the things that fascinated Ben was his cat's telepathic awareness. She seemed to know before he did if he was going to be away from home longer than usual. She had an awareness of things outside his own understanding that Ben found intriguing. Sometimes, if she was across the room and Ben looked at her, thinking about her, she would just start to purr, without him coming near her. A deep resonant thrumming purr. The sound of her purring was glorious. It made Ben think of waves and wild jungle cats and feeling safe and looked after all at the same time.

Ben found that being loved by another living creature strongly enough to turn on her purr – without even touching her – was heady stuff. It took his breath away. He would half close his eyes, tilt his head up slightly, and purr back, but they both knew it was quite useless as far as purrs went.

As the months passed, Magnificat felt the bond strengthening between herself and her boy. She kept feeling the hurt in Ben and knew that if he would only let her, she could find a way to heal him. It needed trust both ways and slowly the trust was growing. When she was near him and when she groomed him she could feel the pain draining away. And in return he too was becoming gentler and softer.

Apart from her role as Ben's guardian, Magnificat still needed to attend to those things that remain endlessly interesting to any cat. She was a hunter and the call of the wild was never far from her thoughts. Since she had been living with Ben she had witnessed the end of the darkest part of winter and the beginning of spring, which had brought in its wake different rewards. The frog-hunting had been stimulating, but now the frogs had gone quiet. Her two tom cats, also, were nowhere to be seen and even the normally ever-present garden birds were strangely absent. They sang noisily enough at dawn and dusk, but they were simply not visible in the usual haunts where Magnificat had often seen them. When they came to the bird feeders these days, instead of having all those bickering rows they seemed to enjoy so much, they filled their beaks quickly and flew away. The majority of them were, in fact, sitting on eggs in nests that they hoped were well hidden from prying eyes, like those of Magnificat, but all she knew was that there were fewer around than normal. She had to content herself with roaming the local neighbourhood and the nearby gardens, picking up a mouse here and a vole there – and so she began to explore further afield.

She missed Ben during the day, although these days when she wasn't out hunting she spent more and more time sleeping, as she got very tired. But she understood now the rhythms of when Ben would be around and that for most of each day he would not be there. It was regular; it was what happened, but she thought about him and she constantly tuned in to when he might return.

At other times he was away and often, when he came back, he smelled of dog. She wondered why? But since their bond had strengthened she was certain that he always would return at the end of the day and she would be there, awaiting him. She knew when he was on his way home – any time of the day.

Most importantly, he was always there at night. And when Ben looked at her in the right way she would purr for him. That special purr. The purr that said it all. Ben was her boy.

13

THE LOOK-OUT

By the time Spring Term was nearly over Magnificat was recognised by local people as the official 'look-out', awaiting Ben's return from school. She was in the habit of sitting on the fencepost diagonally opposite their house from which point she could see the length of their quiet side road leading up to the main route into the town. Whenever Ben turned the corner, his eyes would quickly scan the horizon. Magnificat never failed him. There she would be, atop her masthead, keeping the sharpest look-out in the world. When she saw him, she would thrash her great tail in recognition of him and miaow a loud greeting. As he got closer still she would '*prrrrrp*' at him and bound down to the ground, rubbing herself against his legs.

Although Magnificat was always there for Ben on his return from school, at other times she had started wandering off. As the little cat began to matter to him more, so her wanderings had started to worry him – he had even said something to his mother, but Mum had pointed out that cats were hard to contain, and if you wanted them to have their freedom, this was the price you had to pay. Ben knew he was fussing too much, but all the same he fretted.

One day, Ben got back from school and was greeted in the usual way by the joyful '*prrrrp*'s of the look-out as she jumped down to his level. She stared into his eyes and trembled her tail at him excitedly and in return he murmured little soft-voiced words of affection to her.

As Ben opened the front door he heard voices coming from the front room and, to his surprise, he saw Father John-Henry over by the window with a mug of tea in his hand, talking to Ben's mother. The priest was laughing because Mum had primed him to watch the cat/boy greeting ritual. The priest had at last returned from his long recuperation following his surgery and was very happy to be back in his church – and anxious to know if all was well between Magnificat and Ben and, indeed, Ben's mum.

'Go on, Ben, tell Father John-Henry about that cat,' Mum said. Ben stood up and scratched his back awkwardly. He hated it when Mum put him on the spot.

'Yup. She's good!' he muttered in a clipped manner.

'Is that all you've got to say?' Mum protested.

'Well – you could've said about the frogs, Father!' Ben added darkly.

'Ah. Your mother told me about that. I never knew about the frogs, Ben. Sorry. I would've warned you if I had,' Father John said, smothering a smile. Mum left the room to put the kettle on and as the door clicked shut, Father John-Henry looked across at Ben. He cocked his head on one side and mouthed the word, '*Well*?'

Ben scrunched up his eyes at the question as if it was a difficult one. But then he relented and sat down, grinning.

'She's wicked. She's really ace. I love her. She's going to the vet soon to be chipped and neutered, Mum says.' He paused. 'Don't know when that's going to happen . . .' and his voice tailed off. Ben shrugged. 'But yes, she's really cool.'

Ben's mother came back into the room carrying a fresh pot of tea, at which point Father John-Henry stood up. Apologising, he said he was late for a visit and had to dash. 'But, Ben, so glad things are working out with Magnificat. She came to see me the day after I got back. She was sitting on the path waiting for me to come out and I got the sense then that she wanted me to see that she was one happy cat. She's positively blooming, in fact. I think she's putting on weight!'

As Mum returned from the door having seen the priest out, Ben looked across at her. She looked tired. She always wore her long hair up held in place by combs, but so many loose hairs were dangling down it looked more down than up.

Ben said, 'Mum, when are we going to take MC to the vet?'

'Soon, I promise. It's one of those things I've kept meaning to do. I just need to make the appointment.' She stopped and then opened her mouth as if she was going to say something else and stopped again. She pushed her hair back with her hand. 'Father John-Henry just confirmed that he wants me to housekeep for him now he's back, so that's a bit of a relief. It means I can count on the money coming in . . . All these things don't come cheaply, you know.'

'Well, the Easter Holidays start next week, and I'll be home to look after her when she gets back from the vet,' Ben suggested helpfully. His mother smiled and nodded, but Ben heard her sigh as she walked out of the room into the kitchen. Ben shrugged, picked up the remote and turned on the TV.

That night, as he was lying in bed in the dark with his hands behind his head, Ben wished he had been more forthcoming with Father John-Henry about MC. There was so much he should have said. It was such a funny mixture of things that made her so special. She seemed almost human – no – that wasn't right – super-human really. There were moments when she seemed terribly old and wise and actually in charge of him. But, he realised, as he felt across in the dark and his hand touched the little cat curled up close to him absorbing his body heat, a night never passed without her spending at least some of it with him. In fact she slept quite a lot these days and yes, Father John-Henry was right, she was getting a bit fat. As Ben drifted towards sleep he mused that recently she seemed to be fonder than ever of him and responded passionately to his gentle words and his soft caresses. Mohammed had been right. She was really special.

A week after Father John-Henry's visit, just before the Easter holidays started, Ben woke up with a strange sense of dread hanging over him. All day Ben felt uneasy and he couldn't wait for school to be over. He wanted to get rid of this feeling and to check that everything was all right at home. He ran, fast, all the way without once slowing down.

As he turned into his road Ben saw the fencepost was empty. The second he saw this Ben knew something awful had happened. His stomach lurched and he felt as if he might be sick. This was the first time since Magnificat had taken on the role of look-out that she hadn't been there to greet him. He scrabbled at the locked door, finally getting it open he rushed around shouting out for his little cat. His mother hadn't got home yet and all was quiet. Ben raced from room to room, but there was no sign of Magnificat anywhere.

As Ben called out for his little cat he heard his mother's key in the door and he shouted down to her, his words tumbling out muddled by worry. When had she last seen Magnificat, he asked over and over. Mum's mouth went into a thin tense line as she repeatedly shook her head. Ben, by now halfway through the front door, shouted back that he was going out to look for her.

Eventually, having walked up and down the nearby streets calling until he was hoarse, Ben returned home empty-handed. His face was pale and strained and he had dark shadows under his eyes. His mother came across and placed her hand on his bent back. She was never one for much kissing or hugging, but as she touched him, tears overwhelmed him.

'She's gone! I know she's gone! I had a weird feeling this morning . . .' Ben put his head down again and gave a great sob. His mother stroked his back, gently. 'She's gone – just like everyone else. She's left me!'

'You don't know she's gone, she might be back yet.' His

Mum paused. 'What do you mean "like everyone else"?'

At this question Ben let out an anguished groan. What *had* he meant? But deep down, he knew and he couldn't stop it coming out.

'Like Dad, and sometimes it feels as if you've gone too! You don't have much time for me and even Father John-Henry just said "here have this cat" and left and, and . . .'

Ben's voice tailed off into silence. Mum gave one of her gigantic sighs, but Ben heard it as if from a great distance away. He looked at her briefly, but she said nothing, and shortly afterwards she left the room.

As Ben sat with his head down he thought about his missing cyberdog Shadow for the first time in months. Another one that had gone. But, Ben thought to himself, that was – or should he say *had been* – the fantastic thing about Magnificat. Her love was more special because she could have left at any time and she hadn't, she had chosen to be with Ben of her own free will, whereas Shadow had no choice. But now that wasn't true of her any more.

Ben stood up and pressed his nose flat against the window pane. Slowly his breath started to steam it up until all that remained visible to him through the mist was the cat-less fencepost, whose emptiness seemed to be jeering at him.

PART III

THE KIDNAP

Magnificat sat squashed down, miserable and afraid. She knew she must be in a vehicle of some kind because of the jolting and the smell of diesel.

She was hunched up inside a cardboard box with her back legs splayed out to try and prevent being thrown around and the lid of the box was pressing down on her spine. Her ears and whiskers were crumpled up from lack of space and it was getting hard to breathe. Panting and crying out, heart pounding from the shock of being snatched and bundled up in so brutal a way, Magnificat was terrified.

It had happened without any warning. She had been nosing around in the long grass on the edge of the football pitch. These days she was having to hunt for food to fill her growing appetite – although they were feeding her as normal at home, it simply wasn't enough. As she was staring down what smelled and sounded like a promising mousehole, she heard three lads talking and laughing. Nothing prepared her for what came next.

One of them shouted. 'Quick! Over here! That cat! Grab her. *Now*! She's just right. She'll be great for Rosie. She's been on and on about wanting a cat.'

With that, a stinky jacket fell over Magnificat and two pairs of hands tightened around her. She squirmed and hissed, lashing out with her claws and was rewarded with a curse as she drew blood. But in spite of her valiant struggle, she felt the world close in around her as the bundle she had become was tied up tight. She could barely move a muscle. From the smell she knew she was now inside a vehicle. Where was she being taken? Who were these people? What was going to happen? Would she be harmed?

'If we're going to get that cat to Rosie alive, we need to put it in a box so it can breathe,' the first lad said. The van stopped. Doors opened, but someone stayed with the cat and held her tight. After a while the other two got back into the van and she had been pushed, head first, into the box she now found herself in. She had mewled out pitifully and someone pulled the jacket from around her before shutting the box. She miaowed, asking to be let out, but it made no difference. They just shouted at her and played loud music. The van drove off and after more jolting and several bad corners, the little cat was violently sick. She mewled out again lying unhappily in her vomit. No one paid her any attention. The vehicle rattled along the road while the music boomed out.

The petrified cat had now fallen deadly quiet. Suddenly the one sitting next to Magnificat's box shouted over the music.

'There! Over there! A pub! Stop. I'm starving and I need the toilet.'

'I think we should check out that cat when we stop. It's gone quiet. Hope it's not suffocated . . .' The van came to a halt and the door opened. The lads argued as one of them grabbed the box and pulled it out. It banged as it hit the road and Magnificat crouched down inside, shaken and scared. Hunching inside the box, her muscles tensed, she was like a coiled spring. She had only one thought in her mind and that was to get away.

Now, judging her moment to be right, she used every ounce of strength to leap upwards. Her head forced the folded flaps apart and she burst out like a furious furry fiend. As her front feet touched the grass she came face to face with a large ewe – she dimly remembered sheep from her long ago kittenhood. The flock behind was being gathered in by a farmer on a quad bike and as the lead ewe stamped her front foot at the cat warningly, Magnificat heard the farmer shouting at her captors.

The next thing she knew, the van doors were slamming and she saw the back of it disappearing into the distance, pursued by a black cloud of exhaust. All that was left at the roadside was the box in which she had been forced to travel. Where the cat now found herself was opposite an isolated pub, close to a long railway viaduct surrounded by vast empty moorland with no other house in sight.

Magnificat took one look at the sheep and the farmer and decided to move in the opposite direction. She spotted a long dry stone wall, and started to run along the side of it until she felt she had put enough distance between her and the sheep for it to be safe to draw breath. What to do now? As she had been running she had been climbing uphill and now she had a wide view of the land around: wild hill country. The land fell away on either side as far as the eye could see. Distantly she saw a group of farm buildings further along the road. Perhaps that was where the farmer was driving the sheep?

Needing to eat, she decided to steer clear of the farm and go hunting. Taking her bearings, she jumped up on to the wall and looked carefully around. The surrounding fields grew ever higher and Magnificat lifted her head and scented the winds, but despite smelling many things, nothing on those winds spoke to her of the town, or her boy Ben. She shivered. The wind was blowing in from the north east and it was cold as it ruffled through her long fur. At least it bore no rain. Magnificat stretched up tall, holding her nose high, scenting again and again as a feeling of sadness slowly overwhelmed her, making her ache in loneliness.

Soon, however, her acute hunger drove her to focus on the here and now. Probing amongst the blades of grass, she was quickly rewarded by picking up the trail of a possible meal. Magnificat was in rabbit country and their scent was everywhere, but underlying this she smelled the footprints of many mice.

Magnificat set herself opposite a hole from which came not only the mouth-watering smell of several mice, but from which she heard multiple excited squeaks and murmurs. A cat, when hunting, can easily sit for upwards of half an hour without moving a muscle. And this is exactly what Magnificat did.

The sun was already a third of its way down the sky from the midday peak when she caught her first mouse. She killed it before it could squeak a warning to the others and ate it, tail, teeth, feet and whiskers in the twinkling of an eye. A second and a third suffered the same fate some few minutes later, before Magnificat at last stretched out, groomed a little and rose in search of a drink.

She started to walk, slowly, for she was nervous and everything was new and she had much to learn. Once she heard the cry of running water and she moved fast, leaping in great bounds up and over the clumps and tussocks of moorland grass, both glad to shed her excess of energy and to enjoy her newly appreciated freedom after such cruel captivity. Drawing closer to the joyful sound of a brook burbling along its wide rocky bed she scrambled down and lapped deep and long.

Here by the stream the air rang with the cries of young lambs who, having run off in wild abandon to gallop with other lambs, realised they were far from Mum and wailed out to be found. The sounds were amplified by the deeper counter-cries of concerned ewes seeking their wayward offspring. Suddenly, out of the sky above, came another sound so unusual and predatory in its nature that Magnificat looked up instantly in alarm.

It was a plaintive scream that seemed directed right at her. As she watched, she saw the "V" of two huge wings as a buzzard soared overhead, gliding with almost no movement, wing-tip feathers spread like fingers as the great sky hunter shouted another long, haunting *peeee-uu* that echoed around the hills.

Magnificat crouched down defensively. The buzzard, whose eyesight was more powerful than the cat's, was hunting for rabbits and mice and he had no desire to share them with a cat. Suddenly he dived towards the little cat and, as he flew low over her head, he uttered an ear-piercing shriek. The scream and his closeness made Magnificat aware of her vulnerability and her need for protection. She thought of the safety of buildings and knew that she needed to find shelter.

Cautiously, the little cat made her way towards a tumbledown stone building she had seen near the beck and, creeping inside, she found that part of it was still roofed over and contained bales of hay. Although much of it was damp and the wind rattled around inside, the most protected bales were dry. Magnificat walked all around the building to check that there were no hidden enemies and, having satisfied herself, she rolled at length around the entrance, scent-marking every inch of the ground outside the building.

As darkness fell Magnificat scratched out a bed for herself amidst the hay and, huddled up for warmth, she tried to sleep, lying curled in a circle, covering her nose with her front leg for comfort. An intense series of thoughts about Ben flowed through her mind and she imagined him in his bed and shivered. The little cat missed her boy so badly. She should be with him. This was the first night since she had moved into his house that she had not lain with him in his bed for at least some of the night. She made a tiny, forlorn mewl. In a little while she slept.

In the morning Magnificat woke up feeling a powerful desire to set out and walk back home. She wanted – needed –

to be with Ben again. She knew if she tried hard and scented the wind her, feline senses would tell her which way was home.

But something else held her back. Despite being a young and inexperienced cat her instinct was strongly telling her that she had to create a safe nest. Her night in the shed had been cold and draughty and it wasn't the right sort of place for such a thing. This place was wild and remote and hostile to a young cat on her own. Magnificat thought about that farmstead she had seen when she first burst out of her box. There had been big buildings and lots of animals. It would be warm and safe; especially for a cat whose time was close.

As the young cat stretched and thought about eating, she could feel strong movements inside her belly that were nothing to do with her hunger. She sat down again, starting to groom herself and she smelled the milk in her teats beginning to form. Yes, she must make a safe nest – and quickly! – for the time for her, kittens must be soon.

Much as she yearned for him, Ben would have to wait.

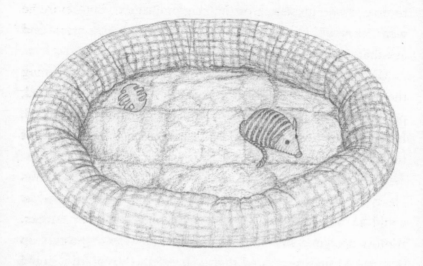

15

THE RIFT

The night after Magnificat went missing was a terrible one for Ben. He felt a great mix of emotions, but the one that cut him most was the sense of being utterly betrayed. A hot, cross hurt bubbled up inside the boy. His cat had abandoned him. She, whom he had trusted above all others, had simply got up and walked out. He lay in bed thinking of her and tossed and turned, wondering how she could have left him like that.

But in the darkest part of the night a change started to come over him. Ben began to listen to his heart and it was telling him that Magnificat would not have left him of her own free will. By the time the dawn had broken and the sun was up he had dark circles under his eyes and he felt dreadful, but a plan was beginning to form in his head . . .

Today was the last day of term before the Easter holidays. Once school was over he would seek the help of Josh or Chloe to do a thorough search of the neighbourhood. But before he went, he would knock on people's doors around the estate and ask them to look in their sheds and garages.

Up early, he put the first part of his plan into action, opening the door and calling her name seven or eight times. Her food, put down fresh by his mother last night, remained untouched. He passed by her cat bed and his heart lurched at the sight of the little ball and her favourite rope mouse resting inside.

He peered through the window at the fencepost. It was bleak and empty. Setting forth, Ben looked into every shed he could get into and begged people to open up their garages. Almost everyone told him he needed to get some posters up and one woman suggested that if he offered a reward it could have more effect. But Ben was close to tears by the time his hour was up; every blank he drew made finding her seem ever more hopeless. At least as long as he was walking and looking he was doing something – to have to stop and go to school was a waste of precious time.

The day dragged by. He talked to Josh, who was sympathetic at first, but then he spoiled it.

'Ben, your cat will come back when it suits her. That's how it is with cats.' Josh sounded exactly like Ben's mum and Ben was left reeling.

Chloe was far more understanding and agreed it was more likely that something had happened to Magnificat. But *what* was the question? Although Ben wanted to believe she hadn't gone of her own free will he couldn't help but ask Chloe in a shaky voice whether she thought Magnificat might have just got fed up with him and moved into a new house, the way cats sometimes did. Chloe swung her head round and glared fiercely.

'You're just being silly, now. You know that cat of yours better than anyone. Something must've happened, like she's shut in somewhere or something. My stupid dog-loving brother is right in one way, Magnificat will come back to you if she can. So it's up to us to do everything we can to find out where she is in case she needs our help.'

Later on that afternoon, much to Ben's surprise, Mrs Matthews – the teacher who didn't like him – came and spoke to him about how sorry she was to hear that Magnificat had gone missing. Josh had been laughing about how unreliable cats were and ended up telling her. She told Ben that if he was sure that Magnificat really loved him, the cat wouldn't forget him and if she could, she would come back.

'The same thing happened to me once and I do feel for you as I know how awful the worry is,' Mrs Matthews said, then crossing the classroom she scribbled something on a piece of paper. Ben opened it and read in her spidery writing:

Suffering cheerfully endured, ceases to be suffering and is transmuted into an ineffable joy – Mahatma Gandhi

'What does "ineffable" mean?' Ben asked.

'It means something so great that it cannot easily be described. Isn't it a glorious word? I bet you'll never forget it now! But I do know how hard suffering the loss of your cat is all the same.' Mrs Matthews said.

When Ben got home, he read the note again twice. It was a funny sort of message and he couldn't see how it could possibly help him, but he folded it up and put it in his drawer all the same. It was kind of Mrs Matthews to try and help him in her own way. Tomorrow Ben would start the hunt in earnest and all would be well.

As Magnificat left her draughty shed she stretched herself. Her first night in the wild uplands of the Yorkshire Dales had passed uneventfully enough, but she had been restless and fretful. Ben had been in her thoughts for much of it, but today she had to look after *her*. And right now she was hungry. In no time at all Magnificat had caught a couple of mice for her breakfast – her next need was to slake her thirst and she returned to the brook she had visited the day before.

Now for the all-important nest. As Magnificat drew close to the farmstead she picked up a huge variety of scents. Amidst the rich aroma of farmyard smells, she picked out many animals. They fell into three groups as far as she could tell: dogs; sheep; cats. She slowed down. There was no reason to assume the cats would be friendly. Or the dogs either.

Magnificat slowly entered the barn and, without being able to stop herself, she felt an overwhelming urge to roll herself on the ground. As she did this she mewled out, a light, melodic sound at a pitch that was intended to carry.

A small bossy tabby cat came forward and arched her back in pure aggression, hissing as she jumped towards Magnificat sideways. Everything about Tabby's body language told Magnificat that she was deadly serious. Tabby unsheathed her claws with slow deliberation and struck out hard and fast at Magnificat, ripping clawfuls of fur from her side and back.

Magnificat jumped away in surprise and hissed out angrily in return. She was undecided whether to flee or fight, but as she eyed the huge fluffed-out, angry tabby she was forced to concede that, as the newcomer, she was seriously unwelcome and so, without more ado, she turned tail and ran.

There must be somewhere in this huddle of farm buildings that she could escape the territorial tabby and be safe . . . Magnificat found a ladder leading up to a hayloft. It was easy to climb, even with her extra weight, and as she climbed she felt the welcome warmth rising from the many pregnant ewes lying in the barn below, about to have their lambs. This big barn was drier and warmer by far than her broken-down shed had been.

Magnificat had found her nest; she felt safe and warm here. Now she had to conserve her strength and sleep for soon her world would change completely.

16

THE HUNT

Losing a cyberpet was nothing compared to losing a real one. Ben had thought that when his mother got rid of Shadow, it would be impossible to feel any more miserable than he had at that time, but he realised it had been as nothing to the pain he now felt. Magnificat had been missing a day and a night and it had been the longest twenty-four hours of Ben's life. Although he, and his Mum too, kept putting fresh food down for her, they had stopped checking it, knowing it would remain untouched.

Ben only had restricted access to the computer at home and the rickety printer had broken down again, so there wasn't much he could do from his house. He knew from his conversation at school that Chloe would help him, though.

He liked her believing that Magnificat was stuck and that's why she hadn't come home. It felt more reassuring than the "it's what cats do" school of thought. It was as if Chloe had faith in Magnificat – just as Ben did. He wanted to believe that Magnificat was missing because she couldn't help it.

He told Mum that he was going to Josh and Chloe's to try to work out what to do about posters and she surprised him by saying she would help distribute any hand-outs that they produced. He squeezed her arm gratefully and ran off to Josh and Chloe's.

When he got there Josh was out with Clueless, but Ben got to work with Chloe, who turned out to be ace at thinking up the right words. When they got stuck, they asked Chloe's mum to help and she was great too, suggesting they made the word REWARD bigger. Ben chewed his lip a bit, but Mrs White told to him not to worry, they would help when it came to the money – there wasn't a sum on the poster anyway. The important thing was to catch the attention of drivers and anyone who didn't have much time; if they saw the big red letters of REWARD they would make a mental note to come back and read it when they *did* have a bit of time. It was Chloe who suggested putting *Please call day or night* and Ben wondered what his mum would say if she heard his mobile going off through the night. Still, it was a good idea. They made smaller flyers that Ben could put through letterboxes and on windscreens and things like that.

It was all very time consuming, but it took Ben's mind off the biggest horror of all, which was that he might never see Magnificat again. Just as Ben had never said it to anyone, so no one even whispered that idea to him and when the ghost

144

of a thought started to shape itself in his head, he quickly screwed up his eyes and violently shook his head to dislodge it.

That night he lay in bed for hours with a heavy sadness in his heart. He felt a great longing. It hurt. It hurt so much. And then, as if he were connected to her, he suddenly felt as if his little cat was in great pain. He turned over in bed and moaned in a pain of his own.

Over the next two days Josh and Chloe helped Ben to look in – and under – all the sheds and garages they had missed previously, usually having sought the owner's permission. Sometimes, when no one answered the door, they sneaked in, and got shouted at until they explained what they were up to.

Ben also started to go round the shops in town. When he ran out of flyers he would show the picture on his mobile that he had taken early one morning of Magnificat lying down like a small lion waving her great tail at him in a "come and play" sort of way. But – without exception – they shook their heads. Over and again he listened as people told him what a nice cat she looked, but Ben didn't need anyone to tell him that.

Mum was as good as her word and took the flyers to places in town that hadn't even occurred to Ben and he was moved by the funny places he saw the occasional poster tied up – something he realised was Josh and Chloe's doing.

Another day and another night passed with no further news of any kind. And then another. And another.

Ben started to spend more time up at Josh and Chloe's house, leaving his Mum strict instructions to text if Magnificat showed up.

On one of these endlessly long days Ben found himself on

his own in the garden with Clueless. He put his arms round the dog and buried his head in his furry neck.

'I didn't know missing her could feel like this. I can't bear it,' Ben told Clueless with feeling.

The dog panted good-naturedly. At this point Ben heard Chloe walk out and, seeing his arms wrapped tightly around Clueless, she bent down and whispered in Ben's ear.

'Hey, Ben. Don't give up, whatever you do, don't give up! I'm sure she's out there, it's just a matter of finding her. We will find her, we will.'

Ben felt comforted by these words, but he didn't say anything. He felt a bit embarrassed being found unloading his grief on Clueless, it seemed almost disloyal. Chloe stood up and put her hands on her hips. Her bossy look.

'I've thought of somewhere *really* obvious we haven't tried!' she said. 'I'm sure your Mum's told Father John-Henry, but she probably didn't ask him to help by putting the word round the church.' She started to pace back and forth, getting keen on the idea. 'People will remember Magnificat from when she was there and I reckon folk like to help.' With that she pulled her hair back fiercely into a ponytail and tied it up. Clueless lifted his great head off the boy's shoulder and licked Ben's cheek making him even wetter. He whined sympathetically, which made Ben utter a strangled sob that halfway through turned itself into a laugh.

'Oh, Clueless, you're great. But you aren't her.'

Chloe tossed her head in a businesslike way and, grabbing Ben's hand, she hauled him to his feet. When the pair got to the church they could hear the vacuum cleaner going and suddenly

Ben felt awkward crowding his mother when she was working, but as she saw them, she pointed them to the study, guessing they were going to tackle Father John-Henry.

The children found the priest tucked away behind his desk. He remained silent as he listened to all the details, but he kept nodding encouragingly. By the time they had finished he had thought up lots of ideas. First he suggested getting the regular church congregation involved. Then he said they should visit the local vet and put a notice up and, best of all, they could contact all the local cat shelters and cat rescue centres. Father John-Henry had dealt in the past with an organisation called Cat Chat. It was an online network that helped to rehome rescued cats, and where you could find details of rescue centres all over the country where lost and found cats would be listed. As they talked, Ben began to feel a little bit hopeful. Father John-Henry had at no point suggested that Magnificat wouldn't be found and alive and well, but as he thought about it, Ben knew at last that he had to ask the question.

'If something horrid has happened to her and she . . . and she . . .'

'Say it, Ben. When you name a fear out loud, it makes it less frightening,' Father John-Henry said kindly.

'If she doesn't come back. I mean if she's dead or something . . .' Ben had got his fists clenched and his eyes screwed up equally tight. 'How will I know?'

'That is a hard question to answer, Ben. Time will tell you, in the end. It is difficult in her case because she has no collar and isn't chipped, but that is why contacting the rescue centres is important. But keep praying.' Father John-Henry paused after he said that. Ben had never prayed in his life, so he hadn't a clue how to go about it and he realised the priest could read that in his face.

'Keep hoping, when you are alone, any time you can. And I will pray for you.'

Chloe turned to Ben and whispered in his ear. 'So will I.'

Ben looked from the priest to the girl and back again.

'Thank you,' he mumbled.

By now the little cat had been missing for ten days and the Easter holidays were more than half over. Ben began to feel the chances of seeing her again were becoming increasingly hopeless. Chloe and Josh both continued to support Ben in his searches for Magnificat and together they visited two vets and one cat sanctuary, where there was no news of any kind, but they were allowed to leave fliers up on the noticeboards.

Chloe kept telling Ben to cheer up and that Father John-Henry had made the announcement at the end of a busy Easter service. Loads of people had said they would look out for her but, as Ben forlornly pointed out, nothing had come of it. In spite of the posters and fliers urging people to phone day or night, Ben's mobile had remained depressingly silent.

At night Ben lay awake, his thoughts full of his little cat. He could see Magnificat's eyes, steadily returning his look, reaching out towards him. As he imagined her, he saw her make that silent miaow he loved so much, her mouth open wide and the tiny point of her little red tongue staying out as it so often did when she forgot to tuck it away. The flicker of a smile crossed his face as he thought about it.

All at once he was frightened to blink in case the essence

of his little cat disappeared, but as he concentrated, he *knew* she would stay with him when he really needed her. She was magic.

As Ben half dreamed about her – the *phantom* of his real cat – he decided she should have her own name. Her name would be *Magicat*. He could sense her approval of that name. Essence of Magnificat, but magic.

For the next few nights, Ben found that he became ever more skilful at summoning up the image of his beloved cat. His magic cat. It was to do with really concentrating his mind and he wondered if that counted as praying. One night as he lay in bed he could see shifting patterns and shapes playing through the curtains, a trick of the moonlight, he was sure. As the clear bright orb of the full moon shone through the curtains, Ben was able to see – or imagine – the exact outline, the shape, the form of a cat with a bushy tail suspended in front of the moon, watching him with a look of gentle love in her glowing eyes. Ben held his breath and watched her with awe. She turned her head so he saw her in profile.

Did it mean Magnificat was all right? Ben somehow knew, in a way that wouldn't make sense to anyone else, that as long as he was able to conjure up *Magicat* the real Magnificat was safe somewhere.

Ben had so many questions he wanted to ask, but he somehow knew that asking *Magicat* too much would dilute her out of existence. And Ben knew, without doubt, that this was not something that he could share – not even with Chloe – it would take away the magic.

The holidays were drawing to a close, but one last avenue

was still to be pursued. Father John-Henry had given Ben's mum the details of an out-of-town animal refuge called The Saint Francis of Assisi Cat Refuge. She had made an appointment to take Ben the day after tomorrow.

That night Ben talked at length to *Magicat*. He kept asking if there was any chance that the Refuge – as he thought of it – would be able to help. Of course she never answered him, but she stayed with him, all the same, and it made him feel hopeful.

As Ben drifted towards sleep he felt a wave of happiness flow over him. He really knew that not only did *Magicat* live, but that Magnificat lived too, as he would know if she was dead. *Magicat* would let him know in some way. Long live the two MCs!

17

THE BIRTH

Magnificat lay hidden deep in her nest in the hayloft above the pregnant ewes, half-sleeping and half-waking. All day, then deep into the night she lay panting and straining. She was a little frightened as she didn't know what to expect. Earlier on a man had been with the sheep below and she heard his dog outside, barking and whining, but she was well hidden. Now, since darkness fell, the only sounds to be heard were the bleats and groans of uncomfortable ewes drawing close to their time.

Waves of pain forced her to lie on her side: that was when it all started. The pain was so great that the little cat stopped feeling fear and just lived through each spasm. Her first kitten was born. It was a struggle at the beginning and Magnificat yowled out loudly with a great birthing cry only to hear the distant low groan of a ewe in the same state. The cat struggled up and turned to lick the kitten's face and nose with violent movements of her tongue and the kitten made a sort of choking, sneezing sound and started to breathe. The placenta followed the kitten and the new mother, by instinct, grabbed it in her teeth and, chewing it quickly, swallowed it down.

But now Magnificat was distracted by a new series of pains as a second kitten started to come into view and, again, after it slid out she licked its birth sac clear of its face until she heard its tiny high-pitched mewling. She chewed through the umbilical cord that had attached the kitten to its placenta and then ate that as well.

There was now a long delay and, after much straining, she had a third birth. The first two kittens were dark in colour, but this third showed through the sac as snow white. Magnificat turned and licked vigorously, but however hard she licked there was still no sign of life. The kitten had silky, fluffy, white fur. His mother mewled out in concern. Why was this offspring of White not responding? She licked and sniffed and sniffed and licked and then, finally, with intense sadness, the young mother recognised that her white kitten was dead.

Earlier she had eaten the placentas to protect her two kittens from predators. If she had not the smell would have attracted unwanted enemies. This was about survival. And so, later on, once she had ceased to think of it as her own, Magnificat ate the stillborn kitten and its placenta to protect the kittens that lived. It was done.

Shortly before dawn Magnificat managed, by nudging and pulling, to get each of the two blind, helpless kittens to find its own teat and so suckle her milk. Once that was achieved, she was able to settle down deep into the nest where they lay, wedged into a corner between the hay bales. As she slept fitfully, keeping her eye on her precious newborns, her thoughts returned to home and to Ben. Even from this distance she could sense his sadness and his longing. She sighed deeply, missing him too. But she had new lives to care for.

For the first few days Magnificat barely left the kittens, except when her hunger forced her out to hunt for food. SThere were mice in the barn, but Tabby was always on the prowl. Magnificat knew that Tabby had both heard and smelled her presence and once, when Magnificat had gone outside to hunt, she had strayed into one of the other barns in her quest for mice and they had come face to face.

Magnificat had braced herself for trouble, ready to fight but, although Tabby had not been fully submissive, there seemed to be an understanding that while Magnificat, the intruder, was nursing young, she was free to stay within Tabby's territory. Magnificat in return knew that she must keep her distance.

There was a wealth of mice in the barn, attracted by the fodder lying around for the sheep. When the coast was clear, Magnificat would make rapid killing raids, eat quickly, drink from the metal bowls fitted to the walls for the sheep and in no time she would be back to watch over her sleeping kittens.

By the time they were five days old, the young brothers could hold up their heads – although their ears were still low down in the way of newborn kittens and their hearing extremely limited. So, too, their eyes remained tightly closed. The one sense that had been powerful from the moment the kittens were born was their gift of smell. By that they recognised each other and their mother and would hiss loudly at anything or anyone else. One day, Magnificat returned from a hunting trip, to hear the kittens hissing at Tabby. As Magnificat watched, every muscle tensed for action, the silvery-coloured kitten suddenly spat, blind though he was and Tabby, clearly surprised at the violence of his reaction, backed off. Magnificat relaxed as the other female crept away.

Every tiny detail of each kitten became completely familiar to her. She knew when either of them felt happy or sad and, even from a considerable distance, she could tell one from the other by their sounds and smells. Magnificat loved the kittens' smell and their little mewling calls, which grew very loud when they were hungry. She would wash each one of them in turn with a passion that made them utter piercing cries of protest, when they would wave their tiny needle sharp claws at her. When they did this Magnificat would pause briefly, opening her mouth wide in silent mirth, while still holding them down with her forepaw. There would be no escape.

As for their looks, no mother in the world could have been more proud. She would stare at them often, trance-like, as if she couldn't get enough of them. The one who had been born first was a dark tabby male, nearly black, with silver markings like little shafts of moonlight. Silver was the first to claim one – and only one – nipple from which he would feed. Her second-born son was also a dark tabby, but his face bore rich splashes of gold and the fur on the bridge of his nose was the colour of harvest corn. Gold had taken two or three days to decide which of the nipples on offer was going to be his, but finally he got there, and slowly her other teats dried up. Both kittens owed their dark colouring and the distinctive heavy black "M" on their foreheads to their black father.

When they were just over a week old their eyes opened and, a few days after, Magnificat could tell that they could hear more, although they were unable to tell which direction a sound came from. She would test them by calling while she was some distance away from the nest and stand back to watch what they did, remaining hidden herself. They lifted their so-heavy heads in a wobbly fashion to look out of their nest and their worried baby-blue-eyed stares enchanted her. They had such serious expressions on their faces. She was filled with mother-love and every day she, like her kittens, learned what it was to grow up.

One day she had been away for longer than usual as the supply of mice was beginning to wane. The kittens were over two weeks old and getting more active by the day and Magnificat was finding it harder to hunt for enough food *and* keep them under control. As she was keeping watch on a previously mouse-rich pile of bales, from all the way across the full length of the barn, she picked out the frightened wail of Gold, rising above the calls of sheep and new-born lambs.

Magnificat scampered as fast as she could up the ladder and across the bales of hay towards the nest. As she approached, she was aware of the scent of a cat, one she had smelled before on the outskirts of the farm. She looked up and saw an old ginger tom glaring down at her. He had come a-calling and his message hadn't been friendly, judging by the reaction of the frightened kittens.

As Magnificat reached Gold, she could smell that the tom cat had picked him up in his mouth and shaken him as he might a rat. Magnificat blew out her fur in a frenzy of maternal anger and arched her back, hissing spitefully at the tomcat as she had never hissed in her life. The tom was not keen to take on an angry she-cat and quickly sidled away.

The time had arrived, Magnificat saw, when the boys must be moved. Already they had started crawling and once they really got going there was no telling where they would end up. They needed to be brought down to the safety of ground level without delay.

Magnificat had found a small annex in the barn next door where a sickly ewe was penned behind large bales of straw awaiting the birth of her lambs. Behind one of the bales was a safe, dark, hidden hole in which the mother cat could leave her kittens while she went hunting – somewhere they couldn't get into trouble, since at ground level there was nowhere to fall.

Magnificat started the hazardous journey, aware that the kits had never been apart from each other for a single second of their lives. She grabbed Silver by the neck, somewhat clumsily to begin with, and he yowled, until she adjusted her grip on his loose skin and he hung limp and still as a kitten's instinct tells it to do for its own safety and she started her great trek down the ladder backwards. For the last part she turned and jumped with him, banging his bottom on the ground as she landed. He yiked his alarm and continued to mewl out loudly. Taking him into the barn behind, she hoped that Tabby was nowhere around and, watching the ewe with some concern, Magnificat jumped over the barrier of bales until she found where she could place her precious bundle. Returning, she made the whole perilous journey a second time with Gold dangling precariously from her mouth. He too complained about everything for the entire trip.

Once reunited, Silver and Gold clambered eagerly over each other and Magnificat started to groom them vigorously, to calm them down. Soon their high-pitched wails ceased and all that could be heard was the contented sound of kittens suckling while their mother purred.

18

THE REFUGE

Ben stood staring through the bars and the black cat stared straight back at him. The look in the cat's eyes was sadder than any look Ben had ever seen on a feline face before. It reminded him of something, but he couldn't put his finger on it. As he gazed at the caged creature in front of him, his chest tightened and he wanted to cry. But he didn't because the manager of the Refuge was somewhere behind watching him.

The manager was a stout, short person called Kitty, who wore a long white apron. Shortly after she had introduced herself to Ben and his Mum, she had gone to the next room to answer the phone and while she was missing Mum had smothered a fit of giggles. When Ben asked her why, she had whispered that it was because Kitty reminded her a whole lot of Mrs Tiggy-Winkle. (Mum had always been dead keen on Beatrix Potter and Ben remembered her reading the stories to him before he had grown out of books about talking animals.)

'Except,' Mum said, trying to pull herself together, 'there are no prickles sticking out of her cap. Although . . .' She giggled again in spite of herself. 'They *are* there in a way. Have a look!'

When Kitty had come back into the room Ben *did* see what Mum meant. Although she had no mob cap – obviously – Kitty did have spiky brown hair that was quite hedgehog-like and she kept holding her hands together when she talked just like Ben remembered Mrs Tiggy-Winkle did.

Kitty's voice was husky and low and her Scottish twang was very broad, so Ben had to concentrate hard to catch her words.

'This one here's been in the shelter for two years, and all day long that's all he does. Stares.' She gave a sort of sad snuffle. 'Stares and stares. Except at feeding time and when he's asleep, of course.'

Ben held the gaze of the amber eyes behind the bars, but as Kitty continued with her gloomy tale, Ben put his fingertips in his ears to block it out. His mother, who was immediately behind him, poked him gently in the ribs to stop him being rude, so he quickly put his hands in his pockets. Kitty turned and addressed his mother.

'See, Mrs Ainscough, the problem is that black cats are always more difficult to home and he's nay young either.' She stepped forward and rattled her fingers along the bars of the cage, making the black cat blink and shift his sad gaze toward her. She pouted her lips and made a kiss-kiss noise at the cat. Sighing, she flicked the name tag under the cage. It bore one word: *Simon*.

'Truth to tell poor old Simon's a wee bit past his sell-by-date. But then . . .' She patted her hair to make sure all the spikes were properly standing to attention. 'Aren't we all? They're always more difficult, the ones we call bereaved, as they're often the older ones. His owner died and there was no one to take him on so that's how he ended up here.'

Ben had turned his head to listen, but now he was facing the cage once more and felt the full power of the cat's mournful eyes focussed on him. Very gently Ben wiggled his fingers through the bars and touched the cat's whiskers. The cat tipped his head down so Ben could reach his ear and at that first point of contact the cat gave a brief purr then stopped, as if someone had turned off the engine.

While this was happening, as if from a great way off, Ben could hear his mother answering Kitty's remarks with 'Mmm,' and, 'Oh dear,' and, 'Yes, he is a bit,' and when Kitty finally ran out of things to say Mum filled in the gaps.

'I do think what you're all doing is wonderful work and I'm sure it must take its toll on you emotionally. Are you very busy at the moment?'

'Aye, we are. Surprisingly busy. People losing their jobs has something to do with it, I'm sure. We've had more cats than I can ever remember come to us in recent weeks. If it wasn't for the unpaid volunteers we'd never be able to manage. We're pretty full right now and I confess it's a bit of a worry – the trouble is that it's always hard to get homes for the ones who aren't what you might call "a cutie".'

As Kitty said this Ben looked at the forlorn cat, who clearly yearned for human friendship. Ben ached. He knew in his heart that someone ought to adopt the black cat, but at the same time he felt as if he was being put on the spot. He couldn't believe he was actually standing in front of a cage looking at this despondent old cat with sad eyes and even *thinking* of taking him home. What was he doing? He could feel the essence of *Magicat* bristling her whiskers in the air above him, shocked at his betrayal. Surely Ben had room in his life for only *one* cat he could feel *Magicat* demanding of him? What, he would like to know from *Magicat,* was he supposed to do? Of course he wanted his proper, loving, real flesh-and-blood Magnificat back and not *this* cat.

It was all too much. Ben drew in his breath sharply and gave a sort of hiccup. He felt his mother put her hand on his back and crossly he shrugged it off. It felt like she was trying to push him into taking the black cat home with them. He hung his head, desperate for some way out, trying to avoid Simon's eyes.

Kitty MacDonald came to the rescue. She bustled towards them, her eyes twinkling, and put her arms out as if to usher them towards the door.

'Look! It's OK, don't worry. I've got your details and where you live. You need to go away and think about this. I know you only came in the hope that we had news of your own cat who's gone wee walkies and I'm so sorry we couldn't help you. But . . .' At this point she smiled down at Ben in a reassuring way. 'We have her details – and yours – and we'll be sure to get in touch with you if she turns up.' She then adjusted her gaze to Mum and pulled a wonky smile. 'To be honest I was showing you Simon in case having another cat to look after would plug that gap.' She shrugged in a resigned sort of way. 'Some you win, some you lose.'

At the last minute, guilt made Ben turn back to Simon's cage. He put his fingers in to stroke goodbye and the black cat looked up at him. Slowly he blinked and gave a great silent miaow directly at the little boy. Ben gasped. He withdrew his hand as if he had been bitten.

On the bus on the way home Ben grunted to his mother that giving a home to another cat who wasn't Magnificat wasn't the point. His mother went quiet and Ben wilted. However hard he tried to explain, it just felt as if she would never understand what it was like losing something really precious.

That night, as he lay in bed trying to work it all through with *Magicat*, he recalled the events since the day when Magnificat seemed to simply disappear into thin air. It was, Ben reckoned, the bleakest and longest three weeks of his life. It had been bad enough when his dad had walked out and his mum had been depressed, but in some way he had felt removed from all that. His mum had behaved as if it was only she who was suffering, that it didn't affect him, so in a way it hadn't. Knowing now that he really loved Magnificat, having her go was unbearable. He couldn't stop thinking about it. And they'd done everything, absolutely *everything* to try to find her, hadn't they? What else could they do?

Magicat's essence was all around him, and it felt like some of the time he *knew* she was listening to him and at other times she darted off to entertain herself in that infuriating way that cats have. Right now, though, he could tell that *Magicat* definitely didn't think having that black cat in the house was a good idea. She was very strong on that. He could almost hear her saying it – except she couldn't talk – not really.

'And so now, *Magicat*, the problem is what do we do about Simon? No one wants him and that's awful, but I really only want Magnificat. What's the answer?'

Magicat looked at him with steady glowing eyes and Ben just had time to see her open her mouth in a silent miaow that actually reminded him of Simon, not Magnificat, before she slowly faded away.

The following day, the last Saturday before the new term, Chloe turned up at Ben's to find out what had happened at the Refuge.

'Mum and Kitty both went on as if it was perfectly natural that I should take Simon,' Ben said. 'As if Magnificat and he were just interchangeable.'

'That's plain silly,' Chloe said, sympathetically, which helped Ben who was still feeling guilty.

But later that day, Ben found himself knocking at Father John-Henry's door.

'Ben! Welcome! It's lovely to see you. Your mum and I were just this minute talking about you. She was telling me all about the visit yesterday. So, what do you think of the Refuge? Was it useful?'

'Well, erm, a bit, I s'pose.' Ben's brow furrowed. He didn't want to seem ungrateful. 'I mean, it would've been ace if I'd wanted a lonely old black cat, but I didn't.'

Father John-Henry grinned, wryly. But then Ben lightened up. 'But it was a bit useful because they've now got full details of Magnificat, and they promised that if she was handed in they would get in touch with us. So that was good, I guess.'

'Well,' Father John-Henry said. 'Cat Chat seemed to think that place had an excellent reputation in networking lost-and-found cats, so making contact with them has to be a wise move.'

Ben scraped the toe of his shoe uneasily against the back of his other leg. 'Father, can I ask you something?' He pulled his shoulders up around his ears in frustration and turned his palms out in a pleading manner. 'Is there other stuff we can do? To find Magnificat, I mean. Anything. Anything at all?'

'Well I was going to give all this to your Mum if you hadn't come.' Father John-Henry moved his arm towards a pile of papers in front of him. 'I printed off some of the advice that Cat Chat have on their website.'

He thrust four sheets of paper into Ben's hands. The pages contained checklists of what to do and how not to panic. Lots of them were things that he and Josh and Chloe had done already, although Ben read everything carefully and saw he could put a notice on the *Lost Cat* websites saying when and where she went missing. That was something worth trying.

'I guess Mum told you all about Simon, the black cat?' Ben said.

Father John-Henry nodded. 'She did.'

'You know you once told me I could come and talk. For advice and stuff?' Ben hesitated for what seemed an age before continuing. 'Mum really doesn't understand why I just can't take Simon on. Am I wrong to feel this way?' He looked at the priest with dark worried eyes.

'There isn't a right or a wrong in a situation like this, Ben.

But if you feel you need to hold on for Magnificat, then that's what you should do. I think it's very positive that you believe that she will come back into your life, so don't give up on that.' As the priest said this Ben felt a huge sense of relief.

'I just can't stop feeling guilty about Simon . . .' Ben sighed and wrinkled his brow again.

'I'm sure Simon will be fine. He is warm and sheltered.' Father John Henry paused and a shadow briefly crossed his face. Then he straightened his back and smiled. 'But as for *you*, it's OK for you to just say to your Mum that you've thought about it and you can't take Simon on. I think you'll find that she does understand, Ben, even though it feels to you as if she doesn't. You need to trust her more.'

While all this had been going on there was the sound of the vacuum cleaner getting ever closer and then the door opened and Mum stood there, clutching the handle, and tugging at the cable with an expression of surprise as she gazed at her son in an unfamiliar setting. Ben, who was ready to leave, decided that the moment of truth had arrived and he should speak now.

'Mum, I know you wanted me to have Simon.' And he walked over to her and clutched her arm. 'But honestly, I know now I can't, I just can't but . . . but . . .' He dropped his mum's arm and pulled his hand through his hair so it stood wildly on end. 'If it's any comfort, I do keep being haunted by Simon. I can't get his face out of my mind. There was a look in his eyes that really got . . .' He stopped, mid-sentence. As his Mum's sad eyes met his he suddenly realised – that was where he had seen that look before! But at that moment Mum caught the priest's eye and they smiled at each other and the moment passed.

As Ben walked back home he felt a renewed hope in every step he took. Maybe the visit to the Refuge would produce a result and he would find his adored cat again. He thought about Magnificat and about the strange reassuring power he gained from *Magicat*. There had been a moment when he had been talking to the priest when he had nearly let it all out and it made him realise that *Magicat* existed to help him keep the faith. She was there to show him that Magnificat *would* come back to him if she possibly could, and she wanted him to know it and *believe* it. Maybe Magnificat had sent *Magicat* to him to tell him this and it wasn't just something in his imagination. Perhaps *Magicat* was his guardian angel . . .

19

THE KITTENS

The kittens were now three weeks old and all their senses were becoming sharper every day. They spent much time play-fighting with each other and at times made a lot of squeaky, excited yelps, as they learned what really hurt. Sometimes Magnificat couldn't help but join in, the kitten within bubbling up for a while. But for much of the day and night, they slept in a warm peaceful ball, curled around each other. Magnificat watched over them with a tender love mixed with a new mother's pride.

Shortly after their arrival the neighbouring ewe, whose barrier of bales provided their nursery walls, gave birth to twin lambs. During this time she was visited by the farmer who, distracted by the constant calls upon his time during lambing season, remained unaware of the kittens and their mother so close by.

After the ewe had lambed it became evident that one of the pair – the tup – was unwell. The ewe called to him constantly to encourage him to feed, but in vain. Over three days the lamb grew weaker and weaker and on the fourth day he died. Magnificat listened to the ewe's calls of grief and her heart ached for the pain she recognised in another mother. The farmer removed the body, causing the ewe to call out even more. Eventually Magnificat could stand it no longer and jumped on to the bale wall and miaowed down gently to the stricken ewe.

The sheep looked up. Curious, she moved towards the cat. Magnificat gently sniffed her nose. The ewe sniffed back. The cat licked the sheep, with a delicate, mothering touch and the sheep bleated quietly, under her breath. In that moment each animal understood the other one perfectly.

Days passed uneventfully and by the time the kittens were four weeks old they were finding the confines of their small space frustrating. They wanted to walk, and even to climb, far more than was possible in their little nursery. When they got close to a breakout they were stopped by Magnificat. She was fiercely protective of them.

The cat's inexperience as a mother made her overcautious, even extending her prudence beyond the care of the kittens. The sickly ewe's remaining lamb had grown strongly in her first week of life and she headbutted her mother rowdily to make her give out all her milk. Eventually, with the keenness and energy of the young and curious, the lamb managed to scramble up the barricade and get out and, having found her much-wanted freedom, she bleated non-stop for her mother to come and rescue her.

Magnificat took it upon herself to return the lamb to her mother at all costs. She leaped down behind the lamb and, fluffing herself out, growled at her like a small bear. The lamb turned to watch, surprised and frightened and, with an enormous jump and much scrabbling, she managed to climb back on to the straw bale to flop down beside her mother. Bleating her gratitude to the cat, the ewe welcomed her wayward daughter back to the fold.

Week-upon-week Magnificat watched, ever vigilant, as her sons gambolled about the barn with their lamb friend. In spite of her wish to watch over the kittens, Magnificat was now having to leave the barn for longer as she hunted. Soon the kittens would be eating food themselves, then they would need to learn to hunt on their own account. Each time she left them she feared they might not be there on her return.

A few days previously, the farmer had discovered the existence of the cat and kittens and seemed to be turning a blind eye to them as long as they didn't cause any problems. Sometimes Magnificat risked stealing the food put out near the farmhouse for the farm cats, but she knew she was in grave danger of being attacked by Tabby and tried to rely on her own hunting skills.

Lambing time was coming to an end and only a very few ewes remained penned in the barn still awaiting the birth of their lambs. One day the farmer came to the barn and drove the ewe and her daughter outside, towards other members of the ewe's flock. Magnificat and the ewe exchanged a brief farewell before the ewe and her lamb disappeared up on to the hills above the farmstead.

When Silver and Gold were nine weeks old they had been eating meat for a little while and Magnificat was hard pressed to find enough food. Frequently she went without so that her kittens might have enough to eat. They hadn't yet been taught to hunt, although Magnificat had brought back plenty of dead mice. She had, on one occasion, brought back a still-living one, but to her annoyance the kittens had let it run away. While the kittens remained hungry, they tried to keep suckling her for milk, something that was getting harder for her to supply.

The young mother knew that the time had come to move away. As they left the farm buildings she was pleased to see that her sons instinctively followed her. The world outside the farmstead astonished them. It was so big and so noisy and the new smells that hit their senses were exciting. The road was quiet as it was early in the morning and the older cat led the two kittens along the verge, towards the broken-down building. None of the farm cats used it and it would be dry enough to sleep in. The small family checked out their new quarters and established that all was well. Magnificat sat back and let the kittens play with each other, so that this place would become familiar to them.

Magnificat called a halt to their play. She had her own plans. Some serious hunting must take place. Calling the kittens, she set off for the distant copse, knowing that this habitat was likely to yield rich pickings.

As the small group entered the shady glade, Magnificat immediately recognised the warning '*chkkk chkkk chkkk*' of two blackbirds, acting as tell-tale look-outs for all the other woodland birds. She nearly jumped out of her skin as a cock pheasant made a raucous screech, then chuckled his disapproval in long stuttering expletives as he bounced his way up into the air and finally, fluttering enough to scare any predator, cleared the nearby bushes. As Magnificat watched him she was amazed he made it over with such an ungainly exit.

The kittens were awed by their surroundings and the strange, strident noises, and crouched down under some thick bramble, where their instinct made them freeze. Magnificat chittered at them to stay put and silently moved on. Having positioned herself several metres away, out of their sight, she held her head high and scented and watched and listened. Never had her senses been so alert as now. Slowly, she tensed the muscles in her body and stalked towards the trunk of a beech tree. She started to climb, quietly, deliberately, her whiskers thrust forward. She was making for the messy tray of twigs balanced in the cleft of one of the main forks. On it was a juvenile wood pigeon, who was facing the other way, oblivious of her presence. The young pigeon was making a purring 'coo-coo-coo, coo-coo' call that filled the woodland air and the bird was plump and grey and irresistible.

The cat made herself fast by jamming her rear legs into the branches and leaped forward. With one quick blow she had silenced the call for ever by breaking the bird's neck. She descended the tree in reverse, somewhat hampered by her kill, and took it in triumph to her two sons, who had remained hidden in their bramble cave. The three of them gorged their fill on the best meal they had ever shared. They hunted some more in the woodland, but the kittens became tired and Magnificat knew that they could only take so much excitement in any one day. She called them to her to make their way back to their shelter and, after they had made a warm dry nest, the kittens slept the night through feeling content and safe and happy.

That night the kittens slept soundly while Magnificat thought long and hard about her boy Ben. She could sense his unhappiness and it disturbed her, for in some ways she had found a peace now in this wild place. She remained awake a long time, with a strange sense of apprehension.

20

THE CAT-CUDDLERS

Ben did go back to the Refuge – this time on his own. Something about Simon and those eyes made Ben feel that he needed to see the old black cat again, but he was keen to explain in his own words to Kitty MacDonald why it wouldn't work to have Simon come back home with him. After he'd talked to her as Father John-Henry suggested, his mum had phoned the Refuge and told them officially that she and Ben weren't able to offer Simon a home. Afterwards, Ben reckoned Mum was a bit embarrassed. Whatever the truth of it, she was more than happy for him to go back without her.

On the very next Saturday, when Ben arrived at the Refuge, he discovered that Simon had recently been let outside in the yard to play. Although in Simon's case "play" was a bit of an overstatement. He was in fact sitting with his back to the fence staring to one side. But, Ben supposed, at least it was a change of surroundings. And now, as Ben stood watching the black cat, he had the strangest sense that *Magicat* was observing the whole thing, as if giving her blessing to this visit.

Kitty MacDonald was very understanding – she had never meant to put pressure on Ben to take Simon. When the time was right the black cat would find his new home and in the meantime he was cared for, fed and watered and, most important of all for a feline pensioner, kept warm by the infrared lamp above the bed in his cell.

'What the wee man really needs is some gentle cuddles,' Kitty said. Ben looked up at her, curious.

'Do the cats ever get cuddles, then? Do *you* cuddle them?'

'Well, yes, I do and so do the other workers and the volunteers, when they can. But sadly the paid staff don't have much time for that.' Kitty straightened up. 'But did I no tell you about our wee band of "cat-cuddlers" as we like to call them?' Kitty grinned. 'They're worth their weight in gold, that lot. They come in after school and spend good time with all the animals.'

Ben thought about this.

'Could I be a cat-cuddler?' he asked.

'Well you're a wee bit on the young side to be left on your own, but if you were to come down with a friend and there were enough of us here to make sure there's no trouble with scratching or biting, I don't see why not! Why don't we try you out? You could go into the yard and give old Simon a bit of tender loving care right now.'

So Ben did just that. Simon was a quiet, undemonstrative sort of cat, but soon he vibrated with a deep, slightly broken, purr as Ben kept up the gentle stroking. Soon, more cats started to appear in the yard as one by one the more sociable of the inmates were let out and slowly Ben began to acquaint himself with the other felines currently in residence. He was astonished at the range and musicality of the miaows that surrounded him as the cats called out for human kindness and attention.

On leaving, Ben promised to phone Kitty once he had worked out when he would next visit. She had warned him it would have to be a regular commitment and because of his age, it would always have to be when there were enough adults around, so it would take some organising.

Every night, without fail, Ben continued to talk to *Magicat*, but in spite of this he was beginning to despair of finding the real Magnificat. It felt like forever since she had gone missing, but the pain of her absence was as great as it had ever been. It was over a month since he had last seen his beautiful long-haired cat. At least *Magicat* gave Ben a strong sense that Magnificat was alive and well, even if he didn't know *where*. If he was never to see Magnificat again, he felt sure *Magicat* would disappear.

The following day, Sunday, Ben found himself sitting on Josh's favourite bit of the river bank. All three children, Ben Josh and Chloe, were taking it in turns to throw sticks into the river for Clueless. Ben had just passed on the news that

Dad and Tracy were moving all the way to north eastern Scotland in search of work and Chloe and Josh had each tried to comfort him. Ben could tell they wanted to get his mind off it by the way they pressed him unusually hard about what they could do to help with the search for Magnificat and he was grateful for the distraction. Dad might be the one moving away, but it was still the absence of his cat that upset Ben the most – and his friends knew it.

Chloe started to talk to Ben about posting notices on the Lost and Found websites mentioned on Cat Chat's advice page and Josh, who was more than happy to leave it to Chloe as long as Ben was happy, edged closer to the water to throw sticks for Clueless.

Chloe wrinkled her brow thoughtfully.

'It's going to be difficult to get Magnificat recognised as she isn't chipped, so it will have to be done on the way she looks.'

'I know. Not being chipped is a disaster.' Only now it was too late did Ben see why people had identifying microchips fitted under the loose skin at the back of a cat's neck. Collars could get lost, but a microchipped cat could be scanned anywhere in the country and be returned home using the information on the chip. 'Could we use the picture we have on the poster?'

'Don't see why not,' Chloe said.

'The other thing is . . .' At this point Ben paused. He realised how weird it sounded after all his pro-dog, anti-cat stands in the past. 'Well, I . . . erm . . . I . . .'

'You've what, Ben? Come on, spit it out,' Chloe laughed.

'I've volunteered to become an official "cat-cuddler" at the Refuge,' Ben said quickly. Chloe giggled and she looked as if she was going to say something, but Ben looked back at her fiercely and she just held her lips together and meekly nodded her head. Josh, who had clambered up the bank to join them, with the ever-panting Clueless at his heels, heard this too.

'And,' Ben said, 'if you're under sixteen you have to have a companion, and I wondered if you, or possibly Josh –' He glanced at his best friend nervously. 'Or even both of you would come with me? Could you face it? It would have to be Saturday afternoons and there's a rota and I have to warn them in advance.' Ben saw brother and sister raise their eyebrows at each other – a moment when being twins showed in their identical expressions of suppressed laughter. Chloe put her hand out and gently touched Ben's sleeve.

'Of course we'll come with you, Ben, whenever you want.'

And they were as good as their word. The very next Saturday both Josh and Chloe accompanied Ben to the Refuge.

Days slid into weeks, and these days Ben's mum allowed him full use of the computer so he was able to access the Lost Cat websites whenever he wanted. Ben found a lot of the responses from people who had read his and Chloe's plea to help them find Magnificat very moving but, depressingly, no one anywhere had even had one sighting of Magnificat. It was devastating looking at the cats all over the country who had gone missing. Ben found it difficult reading the entries where other people felt about their missing cats exactly as he did about his beloved Magnificat. It all seemed so hopeless.

As for the cat-cuddling, Chloe remained Ben's loyal companion. These visits helped Ben, as he found doing something useful lightened his own sorrows. Ben could see that Simon enjoyed the gentle attention, as long as they didn't man-handle him too much, and so too did many of the other residents. Cats had to be allowed to trust, slowly, slowly, and then the reward was great. Although, as he said to Chloe through fiercely gritted teeth, it wasn't remotely like having Magnificat on his knee.

One of the helpers told Ben that the Refuge had their own page on the Cat Chat website, where they posted stories about particular cats needing homes and that many of their cats found homes that way, particularly the older and harder-to-home cats. Ben loved seeing the empty cages meaning another cat had gone, but even so, no sooner was one cat homed, than another came to take its place. Seeing cats who had come in as a pair was always a bit nerve-wracking in case the family who were hoping to rehome a cat only chose one of them. The Refuge always tried to avoid this happening. And sometimes families who had come in with the idea of taking one cat home would end up taking two. But in spite of all of this, older cats would often continue to be overlooked. But, all in all, cat-cuddling was very pleasurable.

In fact, Ben and Chloe discovered, there was something even better than normal cat cuddling – cuddling kittens! Shortly before Ben had volunteered to be a cat-cuddler a beautiful young tabby cat had been admitted who gave birth to a couple of scrawny kittens, one light tabby tom and one a carbon copy of her mother. The special job of the volunteer cat-cuddlers was to handle the kittens as they started to develop so that they would become used to people and be ready for a new home when the time came. The Refuge called it "socialising".

As Chloe said to Ben when the pair of them were sitting in a small side room fondling the two kittens, whose eyes were now open, 'Now *this* is what I call cat-cuddling!'

21

THE BLOW

Up on the moors Silver and Gold, now nearing ten weeks, were growing more adventurous by the minute. At last some of the mighty pressure was lifted from Magnificat; the kittens had learned to kill. Sometimes Magnificat let her boys become quite hungry, knowing how important it was for them to hone their hunting skills to the full. They had grown into perfectly formed feral cats, wild as any other creature born into this untamed landscape, disciplined only in the art of hunting by their mother. They were now half-grown, lean and well-muscled. Their coats gleamed in the sunlight.

When they hunted, every nerve ending, every whisker, every sinew they possessed was directed towards pursuing and trapping their prey. But for every second that they spent in hunting, and Gold and Silver were nothing if not serious killers, so they would spend the same in play. Gone were the days when they allowed their mother to oversee their amusement. She had spent many an hour back in the sheep barn allowing them to play catch with her tail in order to keep them from straying and being attacked. But those days were gone, leaving Magnificat yearning to join in, only her sense of maternal dignity stopping her.

Although the kittens accidentally hurt each other occasionally, Silver and Gold had their own rules so that it would never spill over into a proper, damaging, blood-spilling fight, but sometimes it came within a whisker. There was a deepness to their play that possessed them. They *became* it. As they tussled with each other, shrieks of merriment would be generated, peppered with squeals of pain, and these abandoned sounds tempered by grunts and mewlings would echo off the limestone walls and bounce back from the trunks of the woodland trees. Magnificat watched them harness their abundant energy and was happy for their carefree joy.

The long weeks while the kittens had been growing had mainly been warm and gentle, and each long, sunny day had rolled unnoticed into the next. But sometimes, even when life is at its most ravishing, storm clouds gather and everything can change within a flash.

The cats usually hunted together, or at least within range of each other, so if one of them picked up the scent of a good nest of field mice somewhere, then the others would join the long watch. The same rule applied to when they were following the scent of young rabbits. Rabbit had become Magnificat's

181

favourite food, although the younger cats preferred to prey on the smaller mice, voles, spiders and worms – they being easier to flatten and kill.

On the day that the wind changed direction, Magnificat scented the breeze repeatedly, troubled. A storm was definitely in the making. She called the kittens together to follow her and they started down the road back towards the woodland to hunt.

As is always the way with cats, their progress was far from orderly. They sprang and ran and jumped and danced their way along the road. Silver kept chasing old leaves that were blowing in the wind and Gold raced ahead in jerky, rapid movements before stopping and racing back at the same speed, his tail looped between his legs, to rejoin his brother so he could jump on him and, with a bit of luck, steal his leaf.

The rain started and slashed down in stinging diagonal lines. Within seconds all three cats were drenched to the skin. They started to slink low under the wall to give them some cover. Through the relentless patter of rain on the tarmac, Magnificat heard the sound of an engine revving as a car came speeding towards them. She instinctively froze and crouched low, when suddenly Silver saw what he thought was a mouse. He veered across the road followed closely by his brother as the car rounded the corner in a mist of spray thrown up by its wheels. Magnificat mewled out in rising alarm until her call was high as a scream. There was a light thud-thud as the kittens ran into the side of the car, bouncing off it. A squeal of brakes and Magnificat stared at the kittens lying flat and inert on the side of the road. Not a sound came from either of them. The rain continued to pour down as the car reversed a little. The doors opened and a man and a woman stepped out.

'Are they dead?' the woman said. Tears mingled with raindrops on her cheeks and plopped off her chin.

'Don't know, but if they aren't we need to get them seen to as quickly as possible. Help me wrap them up and get them on the back seat.'

'I thought I saw a bigger cat with them?' The woman looked around, but Magnificat had slunk away in fear and misery.

Magnificat watched from under the wall, terrified as she saw her kittens lifted into the car. She didn't know what to do and lifted her head to watch the car drive away, dragging after it a rainbow of spray. Going over to the place where the kittens had fallen, she smelled the ground. A thin layer of blood was running across the rain-soaked tarmac. Magnificat licked it. Silver. Magnificat moved quickly, quartering the ground where the two bodies had been and found Gold's scent, but no blood. The cat lifted her head and mewled out after the long-vanished car. What had happened? What did it mean? A wave of nausea gripped her and she felt a great pain in her chest. The rain continued to lash down heavily and with every moment the scent of her boys became fainter.

After wearing herself into exhaustion walking in circles, the reality of the kittens' disappearance slowly seeped into her consciousness as did the rain into her fur. She sat in the shelter of the wall and lifted up her head and let out a long haunting wail.

Magnificat started to walk towards her familiar stone shelter. After a few metres she turned to look back. Perhaps her sons would appear out of the distance. But there was nothing.

Her progress was slow. She continued to look back, unable to leave.

That night Magnificat slept fitfully in the stone shelter, hearing the rain beating on the roof and splashing into the puddles. She felt the loss of Silver and Gold like a vice gripping her savagely deep inside her.

In the early morning the rain had stopped and the low dawn sun was trying to break through a thick veil of mist. Magnificat had little appetite for food, but the sound of water had made her thirsty. She lapped slowly from a muddy puddle. During the night the little cat had had many thoughts about her two kittens and about Ben and about her life before this wildness had been forced upon her. She had lost every single creature to whom she had given her heart and the knowledge engulfed her with sadness.

The little cat retraced her steps to where she had last seen her sons. The road was quiet and the water lying on the surface sparkled in the early dawn sunlight. Magnificat reached the place where the car had stopped and she scented long and hard. A badger boar had passed through the night and licked Silver's blood, but otherwise nothing had changed. The kittens were gone and had not come back. Suddenly all of the accumulated sadness that had built up in Magnificat overwhelmed her. She sat back and let out a high-pitched yowl, which throbbed out, far into the hills. A distant ewe, grazing the fell and keeping one eye out for her boisterous lamb, heard and recognised the sound. The ewe lifted her head and wrinkled her nose and snickered a long bleat of sympathy, but it blew away on the breeze, unheard.

Magnificat was deeply restless. As she looked about her the small golden orb of the full sun rose clear and strong above the misty horizon. She watched it climb up the sky before it hid itself amidst the branches of a solitary stand of ash trees. The jagged blue hills in the far distance stood proud against the pink sky and, closer by, little veils of gossamer mist drifted daintily from dip to dip of the rolling grassland.

Suddenly a puff of wind, a puff faint and warm, flooded the little cat's nostrils. The wind was laden with odours that stirred her heart. She turned her back to the rising sun and faced west to inhale more deeply. She needed to be certain . . . and it was true! She could sense where home was, imagine the town and all of its streets, feel the essence of Ben, his smell, his feel, his touch. She uttered a tiny mewl of joy. Magnificat was going home.

22

THE REFUGE REVISITED

It was the end of May and half term was well underway. Ben had managed to get himself on the rota at the Refuge twice during the week, mainly due to the weirdest dream he had ever had. When he woke up he couldn't remember it in all its detail except that he knew that his real cat, Magnificat, was in some sort of trouble. The good thing about it had been that Ben could feel that Magnificat was tremendously alive. But he had known she was unhappy. It stabbed him like a pain. In his dream he heard a strange, high-pitched wail – the saddest sound he had ever heard. And when he woke it was still ringing in his ears. Immediately, he could see the Refuge in his mind's eye.

Ben was due for his second visit the next day, but Chloe had phoned saying she had to pull out because they were expecting family to come visiting. But Ben still felt that he needed to go. He *knew* it was important. He even asked Mum if she could go, but she had work to do. In the end it was she who suggested Mohammed might go with him and so that was how the two boys found themselves sitting in reception.

When they had first arrived they had been told there was a special assignment and to come back after they had spent time with Simon. They found Simon in his cage and managed to get him out and have a long cuddle with him. But now they were finished and wondering what the assignment might be.

The staff had been very busy behind the scenes with new admissions. The biggest complication had been nine farm cats who had been brought to the Refuge in a series of special "holding" cages because they were quite feral and couldn't be handled.

'Now you two will no be playing with those kitties, do ye ken?' Kitty MacDonald warned Ben and Mohammed. 'They're wee wild beasties and I don't think there'll be any taming them in a hurry.'

'What happened? Why so many?' Ben whispered, awestruck.

'Och, some townies moved into a farm that had to be sold and wanted the cats moving *out*. When the rats and mice come a-calling they might change their minds, meanwhile we need to find another farm crying out for some grand ratters and mousers.'

Relieved that it was clear the boys weren't to be cuddling wild cats, they listened to Kitty explain that she was going to leave them in the hands of one of their special volunteers, a young man called David.

'David has a mission. If a cat can be made to purr, then he will do it, isn't that right, Davey? And he has a special project for you, which he will explain in detail.' And with that Kitty bustled off.

David, a gangling young man in his twenties, smiled at the boys shyly and led them to a special enclosure that Ben had never seen before, one partially in the open air with a heated house behind it.

'Ah, the project! Well, this one is quite a challenge. But they are really exciting these two. They have only been back here for about twenty-four hours and they are pretty stressed out, but take a look!' Ben and Mohammed leaned forward and they saw two half-grown kittens leaning their heads on the bottom of a chair, firmly asleep. They looked exhausted. One of them, the silver one, had his back leg in plaster.

David had just started to talk when Mohammed suddenly gasped and, unable to stop himself, leaned forward pointing.

'Look! Look at their heads. They have that mark on them!' David fell quiet as he and Ben stared at the kittens' heads. 'Sorry, sorry. Didn't mean to be rude but it's fantastic. Look! There! That black mark that's a bit like an "M". It's supposed to be a special sign from the Prophet Mohammed.' Mohammed was positively beaming with excitement. 'The story goes that the Prophet loved cats – *all* cats – but his special favourite was one called Muezza. One day Muezza was asleep on the sleeve of Mohammed's prayer robe, so instead of disturbing him, Mohammed just quietly cut it off and put on what remained of the robe and went to prayers. When he got back Muezza very formally bowed to him in thanks, and in return for such

188

good manners, Mohammed touched the cat's head with three distinct strokes of his finger making a shape a bit like an "M" and to this day lots of cats still bear the mark he made on their heads.'

'Hey – neat!' Ben said. '"M" for Mohammed!'

'No, silly! Although it looks like an "M" it isn't a letter, it's the shadow of his finger strokes left behind to remind everyone to be gentle to cats.'

'I like that.' Ben thought Chloe might too, and vowed to tell her.

Mohammed stared at the kittens and as the two boys sat in front of the enclosure, David explained how the kittens had been found. They were in a car accident; one had been knocked unconscious and the other had fractured his leg. It was amazing that they had survived. They had been rushed straight to the vet who had phoned the Refuge once he had established they were wild. The vet had wanted them taken away as soon as possible.

'They were lucky to be damaged so lightly,' David said as they watched the kittens through the window. 'Cats don't usually survive accidents, they're so fragile.' With that he stood and turned to face the boys. 'But now, our special project is to get them to understand that people *can* be trusted, so that when they are ready they can go to a new home where they will love and be loved. Right now they just want to be free.'

'Were they on their own in the middle of nowhere? They're so young!' Ben said.

'Well, no.' David frowned. 'The couple told the vet they thought they glimpsed a larger, long-haired cat. Probably their mum. She had a lot of white on her and had a dark bushy tail. The lady thought the cat might have Maine Coon in her. But the cat ran away and they needed to save these two.' As David said these words, Ben started to feel his heart race. Could that missing cat be Magnificat? Was it possible? How could she be a mother? He didn't dare say anything aloud. But when he had shown her picture around, a few people had said to him that Magnificat could be Maine Coon. He turned away from the kittens and wrapped his arms tight around his body, dreaming dreams. A long haired cat with lots of white and a bushy tail . . .

David was still talking. 'The advantage with kittens of this age, is that although they are pretty wild at the moment, they're so young that they'll learn to trust you quite quickly. Even so, you must wear protective gauntlets and be very careful and very gentle. We'll do it together.'

The boys were to learn a lesson in profound patience as they followed David's lead and slowly, bit by bit, the fierce mistrust that the kittens displayed at the start with hissings and spittings and full shows of fluffed-out fur, began to lessen and the kittens' natural sense of curiosity and their wish to play surfaced. The silvery one initially seemed to be the most wary, inhibited by his plastered leg, and kept trying to hide, but his golden-coloured brother clambered up the small tree in the yard and hissed down at the boys partly in fear tempered with a little playful bravado. David stopped the boys in mid-play, just as it was beginning to get good because he reckoned that was enough, and he wanted to leave the kittens wanting more. But as Ben and Mohammed were taking their leave, David urged them both to come back very soon as it was important to strengthen the bond that had begun to grow.

As the boys climbed on to the bus for their homeward journey they were both quiet. Ben didn't notice that his friend seemed to have his mind elsewhere – Ben's was almost bursting with hopes and dreams that he dared not say aloud to anyone – yet.

23

THE JOURNEY

Magnificat felt full of hope. She could feel the call of home and her boy Ben drawing her on, like an invisible power. She set off along the road, which was quiet to begin with. As the sun rose higher in the sky, however, every so often a car or a lorry would thunder by and, as Magnificat picked up the vibrations, she would scuttle into the ditch to avoid their noise and smells. Walking on the tarmac was tiring and soon the pads of her feet became sore, but in spite of her discomfort she felt driven to forge ahead. For most of the morning she never paused, for drink or to hunt, but walked determinedly on, along the road.

By early afternoon, however, the little cat had enough of the harsh bustle and cruel surface of the road and, turning aside, she jumped over its boundary wall and started a long climb up and down across the sprawling moorland, allowing her instinct to lead her in the right direction. The springy grasses and heather were kinder on her feet and the absence of traffic a great relief.

As she grew more tired her mind began to wander and once in the warmth of the afternoon sun she clambered on to the top of a dry-stone wall and lay, idly twitching the tip of her tail up and down and purring slightly, as she dozed in the sun. A westerly breeze strengthened and it grew cooler as woolly clouds skudded across the sky, now and then hiding the sun, making the grassland flicker between light golden green and sombre dark grey.

Magnificat stirred herself, stretched and yawned, and jumped down. She knew what she needed was nearby. She padded gently uphill and there it was; a long, dark, concealed pool. She lowered her head and drank deeply from the brackish water. Continuing on her journey, sometimes sauntering slowly, sometimes trotting, Magnificat thought only of what lay ahead. By nightfall she had put a surprising distance between herself and the place where she had last seen her kittens. She was famished.

Magnificat spent more than an hour trying to pick up the scent of food and although her day's journeying had blunted her senses, eventually she struck lucky. She had seen a jagged rock raised above the mound of the moorland and on its blind side there were several entrances to a large rabbit warren that had been dug deep amidst the roots of the grass. She listened intently with her super-sharp hearing, using each ear independently of the other, like radar, to collect sounds from different directions. As she listened, so every one of her scent follicles was activated. Using these senses together she could detect a young buck rabbit was about to burst forth as he squeaked to his companions in the colony below. The cat sat on her haunches, still as a statue, taut as a coiled spring.

The half-grown rabbit burst forth from his warren and the hungry she-cat sprang on him and bit him at the base of his skull severing his spinal chord. He died instantly and without sound. Magnificat carried the rabbit to a nearby dip, where she was concealed, and started to devour her kill. Completely focussed on her meal, she suddenly felt an excrutiating pain in her tail. Swinging round she saw a long, low-bellied weasel slinking away. Magnificat was shocked. She had never seen a weasel before, although she had often caught their musky scent, and didn't know that they were prone to making sneaky raids and attacks. Weasels, she thought, were creatures she should be hunting, not the other way around. Whimpering slightly, she started to lick her painful and bleeding tail. When she finally turned back to her meal, she saw that the weasel had brought her half-grown young, who were now tucking into Magnificat's rabbit! The irritated cat hissed and growled in a mixture of fear and rage. The weasel family glanced at her momentarily before continuing to feast on the rabbit. As Magnificat watched, she realised they had expanded into a larger group and, not wanting to invite further abuse to her tail, and with the edge gone from her hunger, she gave up her booty.

As Magnificat moved away with stealth into the darkness, she saw the moorland was coming to an end and she knew the time had come to bid farewell to the rolling rabbit country she had lived in these last months. Having eaten enough, Magnificat was ready to find shelter for the night. The little cat was on the outskirts of a village, which she felt might not be a good place to stop. She jumped over the wall of a nearby field and found a disused hen-house with its door hanging off broken hinges. She climbed back down and headed over to it. Having investigated it to her satisfaction, she settled down for the night. The exertion of jumping the wall had started her tail bleeding again and she licked until it stopped.

Magnificat was just beginning to get drowsy, when she heard a small scratchy animal sound. In the near-dark she saw what looked like an unusually dopey mouse. She opened both eyes and concentrated, pointing her whiskers at him so she could determine more. The mouse was moving around in a clumsy and uncertain way and within a few seconds Magnificat had pounced on him, killed him and eaten every part of him. A great wave of tiredness overcame her, and after a quick groom she yawned widely, scratched at a flattened pile of old straw, turned round three times and curled up into a ball to sleep long and deep.

The next day, when the dawn was still a grey glimmer in the sky, before it had turned pale pink, Magnificat rose and within half an hour she had devoured a shrew, a fieldmouse and another shrew. As she groomed herself the little cat spent a long time licking and chewing on her sore pads. Her tail was sore as well, but her pads were worse. She was exhausted by her travels and longed for the journeying to be over – but journey she must.

The first hazard that awaited her was the village she had seen last night, with houses that almost certainly contained both cats and dogs who might challenge her. The little cat kept close to the garden walls and passed through the village in complete silence. Barking filled the air and Magnificat leaped on a dustbin to work out where it was coming from. The sound continued at the same pitch from the same direction, so it seemed that the dog was either unable to move or disinclined to do so. Magnificat, satisfied that she was safe from this canine hazard at least, jumped down and continued her stealthy progress.

The cat's instinct compelled her to keep travelling in a westerly direction, meaning that the next peril that awaited her was scary indeed: a major trunk road with big, fast traffic that thundered past in both directions. The cat sat on the side of the road for what seemed to her an age and then, suddenly, there appeared to be a lull in traffic vibrations. Magnificat stood up and staring straight ahead she simply raced for the other side.

Over on the far side of the great noisy road she found trees and fields, providing her with a sense of relief on reaching them. This felt far safer than the man-made environments she had just left. She now started to walk and, occasionally, trot, keeping this erratic pace for several miles. She stopped once intending to eat, but she was overcome with a wave of nausea and she developed a raging thirst, so instead she drank deeply from a stream. Soon afterwards she was violently sick and tiredness overwhelmed her as her feet and tail throbbed. In the distance she could hear traffic once more, but she knew she had to stay on this path, traffic or no. She had to get home.

By early evening, although it was still light, Magnificat knew that she was in trouble. She had no strength or energy left. She was close to a cottage and a warm glow of yellow light shone out from the windows, making it seem welcoming. Magnificat spent a long time smelling for dangers when a further great wave of nausea overcame her and she felt unsteady.

The little cat had been badly frightened by how frail she felt but now, as wave after wave of sickness hit her, she went beyond the point of caring about any danger. Her tail had started to bleed again and now so had her feet. She just wanted to lie down. She *must* lie down. She knew she was seriously ill. Magnificat stumbled her way round to the garden at the back of the cottage – the front door was on the main road with heavy traffic thundering through – and mewled out once before a wave of dizziness hit her and her legs gave way beneath her. Falling gently on to her side Magnificat collapsed into unconsciousness.

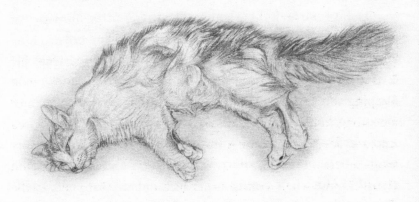

24

THE MISSION

'But Ben,' Chloe said, her voice rising as she flung her bike against the wall. 'Surely you can see, you must go and look yourself if you think that. You've. Simply. Got. To.' She reached out and poked him lightly in the chest with each word.

'I know that, but . . . how?' Ben reeled back defensively. He was agitated. It had been a difficult conversation and it had started before they'd even got into the house. Chloe was so *emphatic*. He hadn't wanted to tell anyone, but somehow when Chloe grilled him on how things had gone at the Refuge he felt he had to tell her. She alone would understand his gut feeling that the sighting of the mystery cat with the two new kittens was the first and only sighting that might really turn out to be Magnificat.

'The place where the couple ran into the kittens is miles and miles away and there are no buses or anything that go that way.' Ben pulled his most woeful face.

'For heaven's sake, Ben, there must be some way you can go in that direction. Come on, think about it. What about borrowing my bike and cycling?'

It was still half term, a point that Chloe made as well, and Ben had been getting really strong vibes from *Magicat* that he had better get out and *do something*. She even came to him in his dreams now. But he was also pretty certain that Mum would never let him go off on his own; although he'd had a bike when he was younger, he wasn't that experienced and the road toward the Dales was a main trunk road with a lot of lorries on it. He shut one eye and twisted his mouth to one side.

Chloe laughed. 'What a face, Ben. Is it your mum you're worried about?' She stared at him with her hands on her hips. Ben puffed out his cheeks but remained silent. Chloe shook her head impatiently, making her ponytail bounce up and down. She leaned forward and sighed.

'Ben! Come on . . . you can tell me.'

'All right. It *is* Mum. I just know she'll never agree! Not in a million years,' Ben said at last.

'Well – you daft thing – mebbe we could go together?' Chloe made it sound as if it was the easiest thing in the world. 'You'd need to ask Josh nicely if you can borrow his bike, but I'm sure he'd let you. If we both went that'd make it better with your mum, wouldn't it?' Ben nodded – to begin with hesitantly and then more certainly. He beamed a giant smile of gratitude at Chloe and her ponytail twitched merrily in response.

So it was agreed. Josh, with typical generosity, said Ben could keep his bike for however long he might need it. Mum was persuaded by the fact that Chloe was going and so, with umpteen warnings from both parents to "watch that traffic!" the pair set off, complete with their rucksacks.

Mohammed, having put himself on a daily rota to see the "M" kittens, came up trumps when Ben told him what he was going to do, and managed to persuade the Refuge to lend Ben their special cat-carrying rucksack.

As he handed it over to Ben, Mohammed said, 'You never know, you might be lucky, and how else would you get her home? On your shoulder, like a parrot?'

As Ben and Chloe cycled down the side road that led up to the main road, Chloe kept putting Ben off by mock crashing into him. Ben wished she wouldn't, but then she started talking and he had to catch up to hear her.

'At least your rucksack's empty,' she said. 'Mine's full of all sorts of things that Mum thought we might need for our picnic. She makes such a fuss.'

'Hmph! Mine never even thought about a picnic!' Ben said. Then he laughed. 'You never know, though, Chloe, I might have a cat on my back on the way home. And that would be a good bit heavier than your picnic.' He wobbled so much when he said that, that he half fell off, banging the crossbar painfully. Chloe seemed to think he was entering into the spirit of the journey and gleefully continued to mess about until the inevitable happened and, with a crashing of bikes, they both plummeted to the ground. Chloe fell backwards and there was the sound of smashing glass as her backpack hit the ground beneath her.

'Oh, bum! That's torn it,' Chloe said. 'We'll just have to buy something to drink at the first shop we see!'

They had been going for nearly an hour in a more sober fashion, passing through several hamlets with no sign of any shops, until Chloe, who was out in front, suddenly slowed as they drew up to what looked like an all-purpose store. It was a small white cottage which bore a sign reading, *Drinks, Sandwiches, Locally Grown Fruit and Vegetables*. They dismounted – Ben grateful for a rest. The door was unlatched, so the two youngsters walked inside. It was silent except for a ticking clock. No one seemed to be around, although it was obviously open for business. Ben looked at Chloe who shrugged and went over to the drinks fridge, calling out a friendly 'Hello?' Nothing. Then they heard a woman's voice.

'Hey, what are you doing here?' the voice said. 'Are you all right? You don't look very well. And what's all this blood?'

The two children looked at each other, baffled. Who *was* she talking to? They called out and the door at the back opened and a small neat lady with soft brown curly hair appeared, wiping her hands down the side of her overall.

'You'll never guess what I've just found. Come round the back and have a look.'

Confused, Ben and Chloe wound their way around the shelves after the shopkeeper as she led them through the shop into the cottage and out through the back door. There, on the grass, lay a mainly white, scrawny, long-haired cat with blood seeping out of its tail looking very sorry for itself. Ben gasped in surprise and rammed his knuckle into his mouth, letting out an enormous groan.

Chloe grabbed Ben's arm and dug her fingernails in, but he barely noticed.

'I don't believe it!' Chloe said. Ben said nothing. His eyes filled up with tears and he fell to the ground on his knees and put his arms around the cat. Burying his face in her fur, he breathed in the smell of her. The smell that he had dreamed about for so long. Ben thought his heart might break. His voice trembled with passion as he uttered just one word – deep into her fur – over and over again.

'Magnificat! Magnificat! Magnificat!'

Feebly the little cat raised her head and looked at her boy. At last he had come. Her boy Ben had found her. As Magnificat heard her name she mewled out her joy. Weak though she was she shivered through her whole body from the pleasure of seeing him, hearing him, smelling him. She licked his hand and happiness filled her anew as she absorbed the taste of him. She purred and purred and purred. Now, at last, she was safe!

But then, straightaway, awful things started to happen as she was bundled into something that Ben zipped closed and swung on to his back. She could see and breathe and smell through the mesh and she saw they were on that terrible main road and there were big noisy vehicles which gave out a terrible stench and the journey went on for what seemed like hours as she dipped in and out of waking. When she was awake she wailed in fright, but Ben continued cycling. By the time they arrived at the vet's, the now silent Magnificat was so weak she barely knew what was happening.

Over her head the vet talked to Ben and Chloe.

'Her tail hasn't stopped bleeding because she's almost certainly eaten rat poison. Cats very rarely eat poison directly as they are fussy eaters, but she probably ate a rat or a mouse that was already dying. The toxins stop the blood from clotting as healthy blood should. This injection of Vitamin K1 followed by the pills I'll give you should put her right.'

'She won't die, will she?' Ben asked in a quiet voice. The vet, hands holding Magnificat gently, tipped his head down and looked over the top of his glasses at Ben. 'No, she will be all right – this time. But she will need a lot of care and attention, young man. Her pads are very sore and her back claws worn right down. She has walked a great distance. As soon as her blood is clotting properly, which with any luck will be within a few days, you need to bring her straight back here for that neutering and chipping you keep talking about – it's long overdue!' The vet paused. 'From the look of her, I would say she's only recently stopped feeding kittens and you don't want her getting into the family way any time soon. It would kill her.'

Magnificat was bundled back into her carrier to a homecoming that was far from magnificent as she lurched from side to side in the rucksack on Ben's back, now cycling as if he was in the Tour de France. As the bike got to within four streets of their house Magnificat, in spite of her discomfort, quivered in her carrier with excitement. The familiar smells of her old territory tantalised her and she mewled out her recognition of where they were and Ben, understanding what her calls meant, laughed happily.

Back at the house, Magnificat added her own eager miaows to Ben's calls to his Mum, who had been told on the phone the main points of what had happened, as the two of them helped to settle the little cat on to her much-loved cat bed. Mum, who had one arm on Ben's back, bent down and, with her other, hand stroked the little cat with great tenderness. Magnificat miaowed her gratitude back. She was so happy to be back in this place.

'You should try to sit by her while she dozes in her bed, Ben, I imagine she would like that. It will make her feel safe. You can take her up to bed with you when you go.' As Magnificat lay contentedly in her little bed feeling Ben's finger gently stroking under her chin where she liked it most, her purrs seemed to fill the room.

25

THE HEALING

Ben took his duties as full-time nurse to his beloved Magnificat very seriously. At the beginning, although her blood seemed to be clotting well and her tail was visibly healing, Magnificat remained weak and frail and for the remaining few days of his half term Ben almost never left her side. On the first night of Magnificat's return as Ben prepared to go upstairs he was thrilled when he saw his little cat head for the stairs before he even got there, weak though she was. He watched her struggle up the first step and he called to her to wait for him and he carried her gently cradled in his arms up to his room. She nestled into the warmth of the sleeping shape of Ben just as she had always done, as if there had been no interruption of any kind to their long-established routine.

Day by day Magnificat grew stronger and her pads started to heal. The clotting agent had done its work and her tail recovered quickly, although Ben was shocked at how much of her dense winter mane had disappeared and how thin her body seemed. Her mane and tail had moulted into their summer look, as is normal for a long-haired cat, but her slenderness came from her hard living.

School term was about to start and Ben became increasingly agitated at the thought of the impending operation that Magnificat would have to undergo. Eventually he raised it with Mum. He was amazed to discover that she really understood why he was worried and it was she who suggested that they ring the vet and arrange it for a Friday so that Ben would be home from school by the time Magnificat was ready to come home.

Ben hated removing all traces of cat food the night before the operation. It seemed so cruel, especially as Magnificat seemed permanently hungry after her ordeal. However, the dreaded morning arrived soon enough and before Ben left for school, one of the veterinary nurses kindly came and collected Magnificat, who protested loudly as she was bundled into a cat carrier, leaving Ben to go to school with a heavy heart. He had a terrible morning, imagining all kinds of awful things that might be going wrong, but Mrs Matthews found him in the early afternoon to tell him that his mother had phoned to say that Magnificat had come round from the operation and was fine to be brought home once she had fully recovered from the anaesthetic.

At the end of the day Ben raced home barely able to wait

for the nurse to deliver the patient, which she duly did. Ben was delighted and surprised at how normal Magnificat seemed to be, although he noticed that when she walked she had a slightly drunken waddle and she seemed strangely disoriented. Her eyes were odd and she miaowed out a couple of times in a questioning sort of way. But she was still herself.

Ben settled down to what he anticipated would be a weekend of intensive nursing. Mum said she was very impressed by his talent for caring for animals and joked about considering it as a career. Ben didn't think that was very funny, although being a vet *might* be a good thing to do . . .

Magnificat couldn't understand how things could change so rapidly from good to bad. One minute Ben had been all over her and everything was safe, then all the food disappeared and the next thing a young woman, smelling of animals and other unpleasant smells was pushing her into a cage! When she called out to Ben to ask him to stop it, *really* loudly, he didn't listen.

After a short car journey she found herself back on the same examination table with the same awful smells as when Ben had rescued her on his bike. The nurse lifted her out of the cage and shaved a chunk of fur off her leg. The indignity! A man with glasses and a white coat came and pricked her with a long needle and then . . . What? She didn't know.

When she woke up she was in a cage once more with lights and people all around her. Someone talked to her and stroked her, she felt too tired to appreciate it and she was hungry as well.

The next thing she remembered was being back with Ben. He stroked her and talked to her. When she found she had a strange bald patch down one flank, she licked at it, but her boy told her everything would be fine. She looked at his mum, who told her that she would be much better now she was neutered and chipped. Magnificat could hear the kindness in Mum's voice and sensed the woman was more at peace. As Magnificat started to drift off to sleep, she hoped the practice of being bundled into cat carriers was over now.

That night Ben had to help her upstairs again, but by the morning Magnificat felt close to fully recovered. She heard Ben talking at breakfast.

'I can't believe how quickly MC has come through this. You said it was a really big operation!'

'It is, Ben, but cats have an amazing ability to recover quickly. She will still feel sore I'm sure, but from now on she'll carry on as normal and no doubt she soon will be.' Mum smiled and stroked the purring cat with great tenderness.

Two days later Magnificat recognised from the early rising that the school ritual was about to take place and, as Ben grabbed his bag and his jacket, she could see that everything was back to normal. She went out through the cat flap as he went off through the door and sprang up on to the fencepost where she was able to watch him jog down the street. She watched him raise his hand as he turned the corner.

Magnificat spent that first Monday checking out all her local haunts to see what strange scents had been added since her long absence, but in the middle of the day she felt hungry and tired and returned home for a snack and a nap. In spite of this, her instinct for when Ben would return from school had in no way diminished and she was there, on the post, awaiting him as vigilant look-out as if there had never been any interruption to any of their routines.

Days passed and Magnificat regained the strength of former days. Her shaved patch grew back quite quickly and she began to regain the weight she had lost out in the wild. These days she was much less adventurous and never strayed far from the estate. She felt very rooted to home.

One day she was on her post awaiting Ben's return, when she saw the familiar figure of her old mate, Black. She jumped down to greet him and he sauntered over to her and touched noses with her. He smelled her. She smelled him. And then, suddenly, Magnificat felt she didn't want him near her after all. She rose up on her back legs and raising her front paw she slapped out at him. Black immediately backed off. Everything was different now.

She was waiting for Ben. Ben was all that mattered.

26

THE REUNION

Ben, Chloe and Mohammed were sprawled out on the hot paving bricks of Ben's back yard, lazily eyeing the two exhausted kittens in front of them. It was a cloudless day in July and the sun was high in the sky. All five of them were panting following a vigorous game of tag centred around the two half-grown cats, whose proud new owner had brought them over for a reunion with their mother. Mohammed had finally talked his parents into giving a home to the two wild "M" kittens who had so captivated him on his visits to the Refuge and who, thanks to the tender loving care of the voluntary workers there, including Mohammed, were fully recovered from their accident and completely socialised.

Chloe propped herself up on her elbow and, shading her

eyes with a hand to her brow like a sailor on duty, she narrowed her eyes as she studied the two kittens.

'Mohammed,' she said, 'why's the long-haired silvery one called Rocky?'

'Because cats rock, of course!' Mohammed grinned.

'And the other one – the gold one – you called Muezza after Mohammad's favourite cat?' She paused, grinning impishly at her friends. 'You know, I heard a completely different version of why the M is there . . .'

Ben watched Chloe closely, wondering what was coming next, as beside him, Mohammed nodded his encouragement.

'Well, the version I heard is that when Jesus was a newborn baby lying in the manger he kept crying and crying. And Mary didn't know how to stop him. At that point the stable cat jumped into the crib with him and let him play with her tail and she purred in his ear and it made him laugh.' Chloe paused.

'Go on,' Mohammed said.

'Mary was so grateful that she touched the cat on its forehead leaving the letter "M" for Mary behind for ever more!'

As Chloe finished her tale, Ben frowned, trying to work out which story he believed, if either, as Mohammed laughed out loud and clapped his hands.

'There!' he said. 'It must be true that the cat is a blessed creature if at least two different religions are claiming the cat and its mark for their own.'

As the three friends laughed at this, Ben's mum came to the door, wearing her slightly worried frown.

'Before we get Magnificat downstairs to meet these two kittens, we should shut them inside safely. I know you all think it's going to be a wonderful reunion, but you never know with animals.' As if on cue, Muezza, who had until that moment been lounging on his back in the sun, stretched, yawned, then suddenly leaped at the wooden fence, scrabbling up it before anyone could stop him. He crouched on top of the fencing panel, wavering, undecided which way to jump. Mohammed rushed across and pulled him down into his arms, chiding him gently. Ben and Chloe both rushed to scoop up Rocky and they all trooped into the house where they found Mohammed's mother deep in conversation with Chloe's brother.

The gathering was something of an experiment. From the moment Ben and Chloe heard that Mohammed had re-homed the kittens the pair thought how wonderful it would be for the kittens to see their mum again. Mohammed had agreed, adding that it would be all right so long as the kittens didn't want to stay with their mum and not come home with *him*! But, they all knew he was thrilled to be given the chance to show them off. Josh – not wanting to be left out had insisted on walking over with Chloe.

'Magnificat must have been gutted when the kittens were taken off in the car by those people,' Chloe said. 'She'll be *really* happy to see them again. I can't wait to see their faces.'

Although the house had been full of the sounds of voices and laughter, and no doubt the smell of the kittens, Magnificat had remained in her daytime resting place upstairs and had not yet deigned to make an appearance. Now everyone was inside, however, they heard the unmistakable sound of her jumping down from the bed in the room above. The assembled party turned, as one, to watch the hallway door – the atmosphere electric with anticipation.

Magnificat entered the room with a sinuous grace, tail high, eyes wide and whiskers bristling forward with curiosity. It was hard to be sure, but it looked as if the kittens recognised the scent of their mother, they had been scurrying around the room smelling everything, but as she entered they stopped and watched her excitedly, ears pricked forward. The first kitten that Magnificat saw was Rocky. She walked over and touched noses with him. Muezza saw this and started to run across the room towards her. And that's when it started to go wrong.

Rocky had leaned eagerly towards his mother until he had smelled her mood at which point he drew back, plainly troubled. Magnificat turned and moved over to Muezza and she touched his nose before starting a steady throaty growl. It was quite clear that she wanted nothing to do with either of them. The two younger cats looked alarmed and both of them started to hiss and make high whiney yowls.

Chloe walked over to where Magnificat was standing, growling, and impatiently tweaked the end of her tail, at which the cat fell silent.

'Now then, Magnificat, what's all *that* about? That isn't at all nice you horrid thing.'

'Yeah, MC. I'm surprised at you. That was a bit evil wasn't it?' Josh said. 'What kind of a mum isn't happy to see her kids again? Hey, maybe they're not yours after all!'

'I'm sure they are,' Ben's mum said. 'The vet confirmed she'd had kittens and had only recently stopped feeding them when he neutered her and Magnificat exactly fits the description given by the people who brought the kittens in, right down to her special colouring, her long fur and that great plume of a tail.'

By this time the two young male cats had run behind the sofa and from there they managed to slink back into their open cat carrier, where it appeared they felt safer. Mohammed's mum moved across to help Mohammed shut the cage for their safety.

'That was so sad. I'm sure they recognised her as their mum when she walked in,' Mohammed said, sliding the spindle firmly into the door.

At this point Magnificat sidled up close to the cage and growled even more loudly. The message was clear. Not only did she want nothing to do with them, she wanted them out and away from her territory. Now.

Josh and Chloe both started shouting at her to shut up, but Ben crossed the room to her side and put his arms around his little cat and whispered gentle things in her ear. As he stood up they could see that the cat had climbed up to drape herself over Ben's shoulder, but her eyes never left the offending cat carrier. Her big tail thrashed to-and-fro angrily across Ben's back. Ben turned towards his mum questioningly, and she wrinkled her nose at him, giving a tiny nod of approval. He disappeared upstairs with Magnificat still resting on his shoulder. A few minutes elapsed before Ben reappeared, cat-less. He smiled at everyone and held out his hands.

'Sorry about that, but MC was really upset and after all she's gone through, I just needed to make sure she's OK. She trusts me.'

'Well her sons are a bit upset too,' Chloe said, looking across at Mohammed and pushing out her bottom lip in sympathy. 'What was all that about?'

Ben shrugged. 'I dunno. It felt like she thought they were invaders. Perhaps after they've been separated something happens?'

Mohammed, who had been quiet while this had been going on, smiled to himself and wiggled his fingers through the bars of the cage at his boys to reassure them.

'I got the strange feeling that Muezza and Rocky got what she was on about, did anyone else get that? Although it did look like a shock for them as well.' He glanced round the room, smiling apologetically. 'I think we should probably go home now.'

The two mothers had been sitting together on the sofa chatting, but at this prompting they stood up and Mohammed and his mum left taking the kittens back to their new "forever home" where, as Mohammed said, 'They know they are really wanted.'

Afterwards Chloe teased Ben about his defence of what she considered was seriously bad behaviour on the part of Magnificat, but Ben said he understood his cat and if she wasn't happy at having her sons in their house then that was fine by him. Josh put his arm round Ben's shoulder and called him a lost cause, a hopeless cat-boy; but it was all right really, Ben knew, as he grinned back at his friend. And with that Josh left to take Clueless out for his walk and Ben stayed home, happy to remain in the company of his beloved cat and Chloe.

Since Magnificat had been back Ben had felt as if he was floating on a cloud of sheer happiness, but the one blight to it all was that he couldn't forget the Refuge and poor old Simon, still without a home. He, Chloe and Mohammed had all stopped calling on the Refuge which meant that Simon was now missing some regular cat cuddles as well. After Josh left them to walk Clueless, Ben admitted to Chloe that he had long been harbouring a hope that Father John-Henry might have given Simon a home. Chloe, who was good at getting straight to the point of things, told him he never would know if he didn't get himself out of the house and go right up and ask the priest straight out.

So that is how, the very next day, Ben found himself sitting in a chair facing the priest across his enormous desk. Father John-Henry made it easy for Ben when he mentioned Simon. It turned out he'd known all along that Ben wanted him to take the black cat on, but at the time it hadn't looked like this was something he could have undertaken as a possible move of parishes had been afoot. But he had, only yesterday, finally had the good news that he would be staying put.

'Ben, when you were in a spot of bother you had the grace to listen to my suggestion, so in return I'm prepared to listen to yours.' He grinned and Ben held his breath, hardly believing his ears. 'So, you think me giving Simon a home is a good idea do you, then? Have I got it right, young man?'

Ben was speechless with joy to begin with, but finally he managed to confirm that yes, yes, *yes*, he did think it was a good idea, it was a perfectly *brilliant* idea. And when, a bit later, he told Chloe, she squeezed his arm in delight.

'I knew it would be all right, in the end, see. I promised you he'd be OK.' Then she said in a funny, quiet sort of voice, 'It was kind of nice that you minded so much about Simon. I really liked that.' Ben went scarlet with embarrassment but Chloe giggled and said, 'Only teasing!'

When Ben ran back through the streets to his home, he was positively fizzing. As he turned into his side street he was just in time to see Magnificat jump up on to the fencepost and he rushed across and grabbed her in his arms. She trilled her happiness at seeing him and he buried his face in her thick fur and mumbled things meant only for her. She crept up from his arms and draped herself around his neck like a leggy scarf and – neck-warmer in place – Ben strode into the house, whistling.

Mum was at home and as Ben walked into the kitchen he found her sitting at the table reading *Harry Potter and the Goblet of Fire* for the umpteenth time. Ben frowned, remembering her saying that she read those books to escape, but he bent down and kissed the top of her head anyway. She looked up, surprised. And then she smiled that special smile that she hardly ever set free and all the creases on her face fell away.

'So what're you escaping from, eh?' Ben said.

'Not escaping. Feeling happy. So I'm reading because I'm happy. OK?' Mum said, making Ben smile.

'Mum, I've been thinking. Why don't I just give Dad a call tonight and arrange to go and see him on the train, without waiting for him to sort it out. What do you think?' Mum put the book to one side and looked back at Ben.

'I think that would be a *really* good idea and since Father John-Henry's just given me a rise, we can afford the fare.'

Magnificat, who had been rattling biscuits around in her bowl, now gently sprung up on to the chair next to Mum and from there she slowly crept on to Mum's knee, where she curled into a ball. Ben watched as his mum put out her hand and stroked the cat again and again. He heard Magnificat's megawatt purr indicating that MC herself knew exactly how special this was.

Ben, unconsciously copying Magnificat, clambered on to a chair next to his mum and, leaning against her, he linked his arm through hers and gave her an enormous hug. Mum stopped stroking the cat and hugged him back. Ben leaned forward and gently stroked Magnificat's cheek, who paused in her purring just long enough to offer him her silent miaow. Ben made a sharp intake of breath as a sense of pure unconditional joy flooded through him. This was a moment that he knew he would remember for ever.

Since Magnificat had entered Ben's life he had gone through a turmoil of emotions which, looking back, he could now barely believe. It seemed so strange to him that he could have ever lived without this adorable long-haired cat at the core of his life and even just the *memory* of the pain of losing her was unbearable.

But this dear, beautiful, beloved cat had taught Ben so much. She had taught him gallantry and tenacity and loyalty and honesty and the importance of being true to oneself. She had even taught him of the existence of angels – or magic – or maybe just how to be brave. And more than all of these things she had shown him how to love and to be loved, a gift so great that it had spilled over into the rest of his life so that he was now able to reach out and properly give his love to others and, yes, to allow them to love him back.

Ben was, he now knew, ineffably happy.

Magnificat had learned a great deal in her time in the wilderness and, although some of it had been joyful, much of it had been exceedingly harrowing for her. Now she was back in the home where her heart belonged, she resumed a steady pace of life in her familiar and fully reclaimed territory. She no longer pursued frogs in the remorseless way she had in the spring, indeed her appetite for frog had all but gone. Although she remembered the kills of pigeon when she had been in the wild and very hungry, birds on the whole were of little interest, except, possibly at the time when fledglings were first on the ground. Then they were simply too difficult to resist.

Magnificat never did understand that the thing that had nearly killed her had been a poisoned mouse, so of all the hunting that she still did, it was the pursuit of mice for which she retained the same enthusiasm, but so far no more poisoned mice had come her way. Her life had an even better quality to it now than it had before she had been so brutally dragged away from it. The moods between mother and son were more peaceful and loving, the way Magnificat had always known it could be.

Magnificat adored her renewed life with Ben. Ben belonged to her and when he bent down and allowed her to climb on him, and she smelled his familiar human biscuity smell, she knew everything in her world was all right. Ben himself had changed and Magnificat relished the intense and powerful affection that flowed back and forth between the two of them. For her, now, life was truly perfect.

The boy that Magnificat had loved from the first time she set eyes on him now loved her back in the same way. From the moment she met him, she had known that he would one day.

She never missed a night by his side in his room on his bed and once, when he went on the train to see his dad, she even went with him and she shared his bed there. Her boy Ben was all that she had ever wanted.

ACKNOWLEDGEMENTS

Thanks above all to my supremely talented editor NoN Pratt who really did help to create the boy Ben and the cat Magnificat and who oversaw their journey together in a most particular way and to the whole Catnip/Bounce team. A special thank you to France Bauduin, for her inspirational pictures, which kept me going.

And thank you to:
   Brian Alderson, Kate Clarke, Michael Dugdale, Barbara Durkin, Margot Edwards, Dr Evan Kidd, Graham MacLeod, Kirstie Pelling, Canon Luiz Ruscillo

And thank you to the staff and pupils of the following for their own ideas and inspirations:
   Arnside National School - Years 5 & 6 October 2012
   Barnacre Road Primary School, Longridge - April 2011
   Bolton Le Sands Library - October 2011 (Schools visit)
   Forton Primary School - Class Four September 2010
   Garstang Library - October 2011 (Schools visit)

Gorsey Bank Primary School, Wilmslow - Years 5 and 6 November 2010

Holy Family R.C. Primary, Warton - Years 4,5 & 6 September 2011

Newchurch Community Primary, Culcheth - Years 5 & 6 March 2011

Norbury Hall Primary School, Stockport - Years 5 & 6 2010

Silverdale St John's CE Primary School - Years 5 & 6 October 2012

St. Claire's, Preston Year 6 - October 2011

Sts. Mary & Michael Catholic School, Garstang - Classes 4 & 5 October 2010

St. Michael's on Wyre, Garstang - Years 5 & 6 October 2010

St. Pius X Prep School, Preston - Years 4,5 & 6 October 2011

And to Cat Chat and The Wainwright Shelter for helping me to understand the issues involved in the sheltering and rehoming of cats and for their invaluable work.

The author, Marilyn Edwards, would love to hear from you, and you can reach her via her website:

www.thecatsofmooncottage.co.uk